Jason Johnson is the author of two previous novels, *Woundlicker* and *Alina*. He lives in Belfast.

First published in 2014 by
Liberties Press
140 Terenure Road North | Terenure | Dublin 6W
Tel: +353 (1) 405 5701
www.libertiespress.com | info@libertiespress.com

Trade enquiries to Gill & Macmillan Distribution
Hume Avenue | Park West | Dublin 12
T: +353 (1) 500 9534 | F: +353 (1) 500 9595 | E: sales@gillmacmillan.ie

Distributed in the UK by
Turnaround Publisher Services
Unit 3 | Olympia Trading Estate | Coburg Road | London N22 6TZ
T: +44 (0) 20 8829 3000 | E: orders@turnaround-uk.com

Distributed in the United States by
IPM | 22841 Quicksilver Dr | Dulles, VA 20166
T: +1 (703) 661-1586 | F: +1 (703) 661-1547 | E: ipmmail@presswarehouse.com

ISBN: 978-1-909718-30-2
2 4 6 8 10 9 7 5 3 1

A CIP record for this title is available from the British Library.

Cover design by Karen Vaughan
Internal design by Liberties Press

The publishers gratefully acknowledge financial assistance from
the Arts Council of Northern Ireland.

*All characters in this book are fictitious, and any resemblance to
actual persons, living or dead, is purely coincidental.*

Sinker

Jason Johnson

LIB
ERT
IES

NORTH

Sink (sport)

Overview

A **sport** involving the drinking of **alcohol** (**beers** and **spirits**) in stages. A player wins after securing the most points by outlasting or outpacing rivals. Style points are awarded by judges for mandatory **contextual verbal combat** (**Attack and Engage**).

Early examples of the sport date back to the **fifth century BC Greece**. A loose system of international rules emerged in the 1800s as Sink spread via **European colonialism**.

The London-based **Professional Drinking Association** (formed in 1897) endorses and regulates official games and represents professional players.

Play

A typical contest has no set time limit (usually lasting one to two days) and will consist of nine stages.

Servers place beer glasses (12oz) on the player's **Start Pad**. After touching the glass, a player must consume its contents or face elimination. Empty glasses are placed on a **Done Pad** for tallying.

Players who spill alcohol on more than two occasions are disqualified. Players who fail to finish the glass, who spit or otherwise expel liquid from the mouth (known as **to jesus**), who fall over (off of both feet), fall asleep or aggressively touch another player are disqualified. Players who fail to seek out eye contact with all other players during the course of a game face penalties.

Traditionally, the first player to use the toilet facilities (a four-minute maximum, monitored) must apologise to all other players on return.

Typical contest (16 players):

Base/Stg1: 5-12 local beers, players converse with at least two others. All secure 10 points. Easy pace.

Ludwig II/Stg2: 6-12 shots. First 5 to finish secure points. Style points available. Fair pace.

Gisbourne/Stg3: 10 beers. Last two to finish lose points. Style points available. Swift pace.

Campaign/Stg4: 5 beers. First to finish gains points, last is eliminated. Style points available. Race pace.

Fishermen/Stg5: Shots by each player in turn until round called. Style points available. Paced as emerges.

Father Geoff/Stg6: 5-10 stout beers. Easy pace.

Larvotto/Stg7: 5-10 beers. First 3 to finish secure points, last 3 eliminated. Style points available. Race pace.

Three Turrets/Stg8: 5-10 beers. First to finish secures bonus fee/privileges (wider the margin, higher the value). Last eliminated. Style points available. Race pace.

Oshkosh/Stg9: Shot race until one player remains or time is called. Fast pace.

Controversy

Sink has been called 'the most disturbing so-called sport on the face of the earth and the one which most proves most concisely that mankind is mad, self-destructive and, worse, likes being that way.' (Freud, J., 1971)

Since 1960, an average of twenty-two professional players have died each year during or after playing Sink. The PDA argues, 'Figures are secondary to the key question, which is simply: Are we free enough to have freedom of choice or are we not?' (PDA, 1962) It claims formal games amount to 'enjoyable exhibitions where self-control, and nothing else, is rewarded.' (PDA, 1988)

Prologue

There's a video camera staring at my face.

A handwritten, laminated note above says,

Advisory!

This CCTV feed is live and HD

It's watching the little flicks of my eyes, the wee jerks of my jaw, the ups and downs of the brows, the tiny, mighty efforts of hidden little Judas muscles. It's on these full open nostrils, on the wet, hot skin of my forehead as I try too hard to piss in this big, plastic, see-through toilet.

The lens is just a couple of feet away, but I can't touch it, can't block it, can't stop it staring at me.

Its job is simple – to show viewers back in the hall that nothing is going in, or coming out of, my mouth

I smile, or try to smile.

My lips are messy, fat, wet, like the skin's been sandpapered off. I flash some kind of grin, some kind of show.

I lick the back of my teeth, my tongue all hot and chewy. I feel like biting it off and spitting it out, bursting blood all over the place.

That would get them cheering.

I go dizzy for a second. My eyes swivel, vision blurs, colours smudge, everything doubles, warps.

I come back. They're clapping.

The guy says, 'One minute and ten, Forley.'

I'm not even dribbling, not even trickling.

I have to focus on this now.

I start squeezing, forcing. I pile pressure onto the bladder from the inside. I pull and push the weight of my stinking, stale guts onto it.

My eyes will be popping out.

My face will be doing the jitterbug.

Am I doing this too hard or not enough?

It feels now like something is going to tear, some organ, some tube or flesh, but I can't be sure of anything just now.

I think, 'Piss – you stupid dick.'

The guy says, 'One minute, Forley.'

I say, 'Aye, cheers. I know.'

It's not the camera, not the three hundred people in the hall outside watching my big beak on a king-size screen.

It's not the people in web world necking shots and shouting shite at their laptops and tablets.

It's the bastard behind me.

The fans are cheering hard, jeering serious, throwing cans at my giant live head, yelling insults about my dad, my liver, my country, my red raw brandy mug.

They like me, these fuckers. They need me back out there.

I could piss for an hour if I could start.

Only the counting guy knows the truth. He's got his eye on the pipes, a front-row view of what's not going into this clinical, clear bog.

They tell me you get them in jails and airports, these bogs.

You can find them in drugs units, in police stations.

I feel his eyes checking now, I sense his sensing and it's murdering me.

I've drank enough to kill myself. I've drank enough to kill a horse.

None of it's leaving. Some self-sabotage, stage fright conundrum, some prudish psychological block, some bit of brain damming up my dick.

The guy goes, 'Forty seconds, Forley.'

I say, 'Aye, I know. Jesus. Do you have to fu—'

They cheer. A flash of a temper. I say no more.

I think some other way.

Pull. Then push. Suck, then squeeze.

And relax.

Wait.

Nothing.

I say, 'Fuck.'

The crowd roar it.

The guy says, 'Twenty seconds, Forley.'

I say, 'I know.'

That army roars, 'We know!'

Some fella told me once to think of waterfalls and rivers and fountains.

Some sinker said to think of the splash of the ocean and waves walloping against rocks.

Some sinker told me to think of someone's grave, someone you're glad is dead.

Some other sinker told me one time to imagine your whole body turning to water, just falling prettily apart in slow-mo, just splashing onto the ground, running free everywhere.

And there's nothing.

Christ.

You get them in specialist whorehouses in Bangkok, these bogs.

You get them in labs where they study insides.

People are shouting what I said last, they're going, 'We know – we know – we know . . .'

I think of saying something else, something winning and sharp.

My face goes all wanky.

No, forget that.

I focus on the horrible fact that the guy is about to say, 'That's it, Forley.'

Okay.

Oh well.

Right.

Stage Seven, Larvotto.

I got to go now. I got to get back over there and show these bastards how to drink.

I'm going to go out there, roaring confidence, sit down and . . .

. . . and I drop my head . . . close my eyes . . . one last shot . . .

. . . waterfall . . . The Foyle . . . The sea . . . Atlantic . . . Pacific . . . The bath . . . Tap . . . Tap running . . . A hose . . . Wait . . . what's it? Niagara Falls. Yes, that's it . . . Niagara Falls. Down the Niagara Falls in a barrel, spilling it all out of me in every direction as I go . . .

Nada.

I push and squeeze more and more. I grip and shove and grope that bladder with every organ and cord and bone and muscle that moves. I ram my eyelids and push until my head shoulders go up, until my face aches, until the crowd whoops at a guy who looks like he's shitting out a fucking Volvo.

And zero.

The guy says, 'And you're out, Forley.'

I say, 'Right, cheers.'

And that's it.

I shake my little damp blob, so angry I could rip it off.

I try to relax my mug. I try to make it look like I've just had some major relief. They can't really know if I did or not, these unsharp fans, these blunted crackpots.

I look at the cam as I swing my sprout like it's a power hose, a warhead – my timid dough knob, my soggy little mushroom.

I swing nothing.

I have failed here.

Zip. I wash. I splash.

The crowd clap like seals as I walk back into the hall all Tony Montana.

I put a fist up.

I shout, 'Get us a drink, ya BASTARDS.'

They explode like F1s, they roar like thunder.

They like me, these sodden freaks, these wet maniacs. They like seeing me do this thing for them.

My bladder is so packed I can't even tell you.

If it splits, I'll drown inside out.

Chapter One

My name is Baker Forley and I am not an alcoholic.

I am not sitting in a circle with a bunch of wasters crying my lamps out and telling you about waking up with blood on my face and not knowing how it got there.

I am not going to tell you some sticky shite about spitting on a cop and getting hitched to some painted, unwrapped doll after a blowjob in a chip shop.

I'm not going to tell you I like a hardcore juice at 7.15am and that I would swap any and every meal for a half bottle of vodka, that I ring-fence drinking money and can't care about the kids.

Not even that I don't mind who my friends are as long as they come with gusto to that shouty, serious place we go.

I am not that guy. I know that guy, and he's not me. I'm not the addict, not the guy who seeks only to repeat the feeling. I'm the pro, the sinker, the guy who seeks only to improve the performance.

I got the call for this invitation-only event in Mallorca, Spain. I was the last guy to be asked, the new guy, the outsider. One guy dropped out with some heart issue, and they called me to fill the seat. Only six months on the amateur circuit in Ireland, only two months as a pro in London, and they called me.

Serious.

It was an invite to a competition called the Bullfight. It's a pretty messy one. It always gets people complaining. Last time round, one player took a ruptured aneurysm. Another guy got sunburned to shite but wouldn't leave his seat. The paramedics gave him saline and bandaged him up as he did whiskey shots in beer-branded boxers. The aneurysm fella died.

All the competitions have names: the Bank Robbery, Horizontal Thursday, the Throne Kicker, Retox, Organ Blender, Yeast Beastie, the Farce, Throat Fire. And the players have names too: Iron Bladder, Black Breath, Honky Eyes, Whisper Bleed, Sinker Soldier . . . whatever.

The Bullfight is one of the big ones, one of the ones the fans travel to from anywhere. It's every two years in Palma, the biggest city on the island. Nine stages, sixteen seats.

It was good to get asked. It showed I was starting to go places, that I was getting noticed as a pro, that the training was paying off.

I'd known for a while my technique was improving, but my likeability profile was also on the rise. The fans had been taking to me, to my persona, even though I appeared pretty cold most of the time.

My American coach-manager Ratface reckons I've got appeal because I never drink outside a competition. He says when I go to parties it's like a biker turning up on a bicycle – it's unexpected, interesting. No one expects a pro drinker not to drink. Ratface makes sure I get to a lot of social events to keep myself visible, to show myself off with no glug in my hand.

I get asked about social drinking all the time and I just say I don't do it. I smile when I say it, but just for a second. I only ever smile just for a second. That's about as long as I can smile for. My face doesn't fold too easily. I say I don't drink for fun, I drink for sport. Then I flash a smile.

Me and little Ratface took a flight to Palma for the Bullfight. He worked on pepping me up for the whole trip, coaching me, jamming hard, fizzy words into my head from all sorts of angles to make them stick.

He leaned into my dainty chicken dinner, said 'Relentless.'

He came back from the bog and that snappy face sprung over my shoulder, whispered 'Tenacious.'

His cunty countenance shot into view as I read the back of the sick bag, said 'Not dead can't quit.'

I said, 'Aye, fuck's sake, I know.'

And that's all I said. I just let him slabber on, let the wisdom fall on anyone's ears who wanted it. I did appreciate it and all, but my brain was away on one. It kept saying mad blundering, jump-the-gun stuff like, 'Here we go, Baker – here comes the big time,' and I had to tell it wise up.

I wriggled my toes and thought about the slow stink of cabin food coming my way. I looked out and thought about surfing on the clouds, about the plane slamming into another plane at some almighty combined speed.

I sat there thinking about how some recorded message and wide-faced steward had told me to whistle if in the ocean. I thought how I'd heard, *'Fit your own mask first'*. I thought about how I was going to brace my body for this Bullfight.

I thought about what it must be like to work on that hurtling metal tube, about how the toilets operate, about where the stuff goes, about signing autographs for drunk women, about coming back in first class, about 'Here we go, Baker – here comes the big time.'

And Ratface just kept on jabbering stuff about tactics, about the strategy he'd used at his first Bullfight, and I just heard mush and watched that overbite chop up words.

Excited people really need to see themselves, to hear themselves.

I nodded a few times, turned away, slid some shades onto my dead-man face and fell asleep over France or somewhere.

Chapter Two

Palma is total tourist town, all cruise ship couples, easy-clean bars and non-stick clubs. It's all conveyor-belt restaurants and blow-in shift workers, all face and no teeth. Tourists rule the roost. They know what they want, what they love, and they love the Bullfight.

The sinkers bring in the crowds. They bring in people who jam pissed hands into cluttered pockets to buy more and more booze all over the town.

And when money gets spent on booze, it gets spent on burgers and taxis and magnets and roses and beds and T-shirts and rubbers and vajazzles and poker and ice cream and acres of bling and towels and tips and timeshares and doctors and a hundred thousand thrills and happy endings.

Big red posters are bursting about the Bullfight all over the airport, calling everyone to the city square in silent shouts. The image is a muscle-bound black bull, its nose tapered down like a hot shot glass, steam weaving from the top and slaloming between its bullet eyes and shining, razor-edged horns.

It's so OTT I'm embarrassed for myself.

The dregs of media are waiting for the last sinkers to arrive. Luckily I don't get too easily recognised. I don't have a trademark, no jeans made out of beer caps like some German guy I saw. I don't have, for example, a girl on my arm who has 'Jack Daniels' tattooed on her face. And I don't even know any girl with hard, horizontal, bolted-on tits and none who strut them around, hip flask jammed between, a G-string and mile-long boots below.

I pull my yellow 'I Heart Derry Very Much' cap down low and fast walk on through, faster than Ratface. Balls to him and his shite about attracting attention.

One little reporter catches my eye and walks behind me. It's a wee bit weird. He comes to the side, points at my face. He chews his pen, points again, still walking.

I'm thinking, 'Go away, you wee shite.'

He's sure he's seen me somewhere before, but not very sure of it.

Someone takes my picture and I smile for one second.

The reporter says, 'Do you believe you have the experience to win the Bullfight.'

His face says he's hoping my name will come to him, or at least that I'll be all nice if it doesn't.

I say, 'Yep. That's what I'm here to do, my friend.'

'You're . . . Baker Forley right? From Ireland? The Reactor?'

'Aye, the same.'

'Okay, Baker. Great. So do you have any words for Bad Buck? You know he called you a, what was it, "A flash in the piss pan"? You heard that? You read the blogs, Baker?'

'Nah,' I say. 'I don't bother with that stuff, to be honest. I've got no words for anyone. We'll just see what happens.'

And I smile at him, that off-white burst. He smiles back and stops walking.

Ratface catches up, pushes me into a cab by the arse, always trying to make me look all urgent in front of the press. We speed off to the hotel.

He says, 'I'm pissed off, Baker. You say you're talking to no press then you talk to some guy from some dumb little English ex-pat paper? The TV cameras are looking for you and you go and do that?'

I say, 'I'll be around tomorrow. I'll be around *mañana*. And you never need to touch my arse, right? I've said it before. Don't touch my arse.'

He says, 'The sponsors don't like this shit, man. You need to get your act together. We can't screw around any longer. It's taken a lot of work to get here so don't mess this up. This is opportunity, man. Why can't you see that? And when did I ever touch your drunk ginger ass?'

Aye. Ginger hair.

Right enough.

I'm going to get burned shitless on this island.

There's always two crowds at sinkers' hotels – fans and protesters, lovers and haters, the yin and yang.

Protesters wave placards calling for a ban and shout statistics about the sport and the lifespan of livers and the empty, endless void of death, and stuff like that.

They're mostly with that pressure group, that one that's mad about drink, that wants everyone in the Pro Drinking Association to go to jail. They're everything from Christians to keep-fit freaks, weeping chat-show mothers, recovering alcoholics, disgruntled brewers, people with scars and biological function issues, people with incontinence pads, muddled memories, bad dreams, hard money problems.

They're all about the numbers, about getting leaflets into

hands, about saying if you knew what they had to say then you would join them. They talk about the suicides – knives, guns, pills, trains, ropes, roofs, rivers – the dead ends for the young people getting involved in the sport, as if there's something I can do about that.

The fans – they're usually all blocked – wave bottles of whiskey and beer and whoop and laugh and shout your name and yell shite about free trade and show their tits and dicks and ask you to sign them or they stick a tongue out and pour something on it and shake. They always end up naked, dancing, laughing or fighting point-blank with the people who despise them, who fear for them.

Local news broadcasts always fire up the old debate and let everyone have their say about the rights and wrongs of pro drinking, about the sport being borderline everything, about how it was once stupidly seen as manly, once courageous, once glamorous, about how it was once fearsome, about it being pathetic now, about it being fun.

Today the protesters are all about the new internet channel, ProDrink TV. There's a banner saying more fans are dying because they're trying to match the pros, trying to neck glass for glass with them as they watch competitions online. They're saying the sport is disgraced and dying and has turned to webcasting to find fresh meat. They're shouting now that the PDA is 'marketing madness' into every home, that it's 'violating viewers, doling out damage, advertising addiction and selling suicide worldwide'.

I keep my head down as our cab pulls up. I don't want to debate this stuff. I was asked about it – this copycat drinking – in an interview I gave in London. I said it's all voluntary – suicide, drinking, whatever. I said it's freedom – freedom of expression, freedom of speech, freedom to suck, spit, swallow, say or shout anything you want, freedom of whatever it is you want to do with your mouth.

Some fans emailed to say I spoke well and sent me poems and pictures of them drinking or asleep or of their arses, of whiskey or flags.

And some protesters wrote to tell me I've got a mop for a heart and a drenched brain and that drink isn't freedom but prison. They sent me poems and pictures of weird babies and flags and dead faces and homeless people on their hole looking up at the camera.

I didn't write back to any of them because that would be making room in my life for all of that, and I can't give room in my life away so easily. That debate isn't my debate. Side effects are not my debate, alcoholism is not my debate.

I just tell them I am no alcoholic because I do not do double-think, I do not want to drink more and less at exactly the same time.

I have no mixed emotions.

I don't want to drink at all.

Me and Ratface get out and shoulder through this hot, loud crowd, shades on, heads down, not being part of any of the stuff.

He winks at the receptionist in the hotel, a yellowed eye, a diluted twinkle.

She's pretty and lean and her arms shine. She's seen a thousand stupid bastards in baseball caps and sunglasses like us before.

Ratface says, 'This is Baker Forley, pro drinker.' He slides ten euro over the counter like he's a secret agent.

He doesn't hear me sigh.

I drink some water.

'Baker will be checking in under the name of Mr Bullfight,' he says. 'If the press come sniffing around or any of those freaks outside come sniffing around looking for Baker Forley, you say there's no Baker Forley here. Right?'

He winked again.

She says, 'We already have two Mr Bullfights. You got another name?'

Chapter Three

You get an official nickname when you turn pro, and they called me the Reactor. I don't know why. One day your name appears different on the PDA website than it did the day before. One day there's something slammed between the words your parents made yours as a pure newborn.

You look at it thinking how alien it is.

Instead of Baker Forley, one day you find out you're Baker 'the Reactor' Forley. I didn't get too excited, to be honest.

Then you get a call from your coach-manager to talk it over as a brand, to talk about your second christening, about another one you'd fuck all say in.

Ratface said he thought it was great, said I was on my way. But then he admitted it was shite. He rang me at 4am from his beach house in Florida - which I know for a fact is a caravan in Pennsylvania - and tried to tell me to think big. He said to think of a giant concrete nuclear reactor quaking with lethal power and dominating everything around it with the reputation of Hell itself. Chernobyl, he meant.

Ratface said Chernobyl had a positive point to it, if you think of it strictly in terms of power, if you ignore the disaster.

We paused for a while and he said he'd see if he could talk to someone about getting some work done on the Reactor thing, but he wasn't hopeful.

He says, 'I'm not happy if you don't feel it clicking with your DNA, Baker.'

I say, 'Ah sure, it's no big deal.'

'Well,' he says, 'I'm going to talk to those dildos at the PDA. That damn pretty committee, man.'

He always called the PDA the 'pretty committee' because it just sits there trying to look good. It doesn't really do anything that doesn't make it money or win it more fans or carve it out some scarce PR.

Ratface rang back later saying said I'd forevermore be known as the Reactor because it was already on the internet.

He goes, 'This is the single worst moment of my life as a manager.'

I told him it was grand, it was just a matter of starting to own it.

Some pro from Canada called Charlie 'Honky Eyes' Hutchinson called me that day too, introduced himself, said he'd always been baffled by nicknames.

He says, 'Maybe yours is something to do with the way they think of your style. Like, maybe they're thinking you might not be a natural pacesetter, but more of a follower. You sit in a guy's slipstream and then, suddenly – react! You attack! You're like a lion in the grass. Like Lance Armstrong, all fresh-blooded.'

I say, 'Aye, I suppose.'

We agreed my nickname was balls, but I said it wouldn't be troubling me. I said I felt everyone was worrying about it more than me.

Honky Eyes said he felt he'd been through a similar thing with people worrying a lot about him the day he got his nickname, but the difference was his really did trouble him. He wondered what the PDA had been trying to say when they came up with it, about what was between the lines.

He says, 'You ever hear of Honky Eyes before you heard of me?'

'No.'

'Same. I mean, what the fuck man?'

I say, 'It's how black guys used to insult white guys in the seventies in New York and all, isn't it?'

'Yeah, it is. That's what it is.'

I didn't know if Charlie 'Honky Eyes' was black or white at that stage.

He goes, 'And FYI, I'm a black man with black man's dark eyes. What the hell are they thinking, for Christ's sake? How can I have Honky Eyes? What are they saying? It freaks me out.'

I said he should forget it.

There's a Finnish guy called the Puncher, an English guy called Fireking, an Aussie called BarBell, a Swiss called Rhubarb Bag. There are better names out there, great names.

But, as I say, whatever.

Reactor is dead on.

If I'm dead honest, I kind of thought Reactor was as if I was being underestimated, as if I was being labelled as the man who's always behind. And that's a kind of a challenge in itself.

The name could only become what, in the end, I made it become.

I told Honky Eyes my plan was to make the Reactor the name the fans shouted louder than any other. He said that was a good plan. I said I couldn't let it influence me in a bad way. If I did that then I'd be worrying all the time about what the other sinkers thought about me or said about me, and my whole game would turn to shite.

I said a guy's got to stay focused, face them all down. They can call me whatever they want. Whatever it is, I've been called worse.

Honky Eyes says, 'Yeah,' but he was still thinking about his own name at the time.

Chapter Four

Ratface and me, at the St Regis Mallorca, go to our rooms. There's a welcome pack on the bed, an invite to travel about the place on a bus stacked with chilled sangria and flying a big flag.

There's an invite from the mayor asking us to eat with him tonight. He's signed it with a happy face and written 'Best paella in Palma!!!' He's a three exclamation mark man, a man who would grin a lot.

Ratface had told me hooking up with the mayor would be one of the showpiece events, that all the media would be there to see the pros eat paella and sink sangria because that's what people wanted.

He calls me on the room phone.

I drink water and he talks.

'You got to go and do the Spanish thing Baker,' he says. 'Go there and just totally refuse to drink any sangria. Tell them you don't drink alcohol socially and smile falsely like you do. Smile beside the mayor. He's a smiley bastard. It'll look great, get you talked about. It's gold dust. You have to show your face, man. I know how this shit works.'

I'm not mad about the idea. I can't remember what paella is exactly, but I think it's meaty, carby. Mayor-quality paella could only be good. But I've already been packing myself heavy with carbs for twenty-four hours.

I'm deciding right now.

No.

If I'm going to do eating, I'm doing it alone.

I need to adjust to the climate, sweat it out a wee bit in the heat, line my stomach, boost up on Vitamin B, hydrate, take an early night, get used to this new pressure level.

I tell Ratface I'm not going to make it.

He says, 'You're an asshole, Baker. We just got some great sponsorship and you're already cutting out on the deal.'

He lied. My sponsorship's not great. I've got a tie-in with a little known and totally shit vodka-based Irish energy drink – *A$$tro* – and a singles bar in Derry called Darby O'Kills, which is a pretty upsetting place to spend an evening.

I'm supposed to attend all so-called positive publicity events associated with competitions I'm in, as long as my attendance isn't unreasonable – meaning as long as I'm able to stand up. And I'm supposed to drink *A$$tro* publicly which, like everyone else in the world, I will never do.

Truth is Ratface did get the new deal alone. I'd been told he was pretty good at that kind of stuff, at building up excitement in people, at getting them to hand over money. Everyone has been backing away from pro drinking, all the big money is long gone and, to be fair, he did well to get anything.

I say, 'Here, tomorrow's a big day. The sponsors won't want to know me if I don't do well at the game. You can forget tonight, like. I have to do some serious focusing.'

He comes round to my way of thinking. He knows I'm making sense. He knows I didn't sign up to be a publicity monkey, that I signed up to win, to be a champion, that this is a moment for me.

He knows I have workable ambition somewhere, that I want to win money.

If I do well or even win the Bullfight, it'll help clear the debts and put me in contention for the World Championships next year, for a shot at the Big Gold Bottle.

If I chuck up, if I jesus, if I fall over or spill or something else stupid then I really will be that 'flash in the piss pan' and I'll be lucky to ever get an invite again.

I need to strike a light now I'm here. It's time. Pro drinking is all about pacing and balance, waiting for the right time to reach out and take the risks, synchronising your organs with the opportunities.

A fella can only take so many heavy hits.

This was the time for the Reactor to get ready.

My guts had been hurting for a couple of days earlier in the week. Hard and soft in the wrong places, organ edges sticking out of my skin. I'd flushed my engine out over and over and ran some salts and vits through.

I can only hope it's all sturdy because a storm is coming.

Do you know what I can do?

I can start from dry to dropping shots in just over three seconds, shot after shot after shot, not missing a beat. Can you?

As your body is saying 'you need to not do this,' I move up a gear, dropping them in two – controlled, controlled, controlled.

It takes twenty seconds before you're yelling inside, before you're thinking it's all going to come shooting back up your throat. You're already thinking about the force of the ejection, about the mess, the embarrassment, the fantastic stupidity of what you've got yourself in to.

And I'm thinking *commit, down, clear – commit, down, clear.*

And anyone watching is thinking how someone better start opening that second bottle because I'm coming its way.

And on I go.

It's the ultimate in self-control.

I'm the hard-practised, fine-tuned version of that man from the pubs of way back, the die-young mad bastard you've seen turning wine into water, that stupid dropout fucker wasting his promise glass by glass, who never seems to question it.

And at the end of the night, then or now, I'm the last man standing, the unfloored, the holder, the absorber, the experienced, the boldest, the frankly firmest human construction in the place.

I gave up quitting after the talent hit me, when things got clear. These days, for me, it's all about ambition, not oblivion. Ambition, now or never.

They say as a career, pro drinking is like being a cheap hooker, 24/7 for all your short years on the stool, that it's bang after bang after bang and no one loves you, that sooner or later nothing gets to mean anything, that no one wants to bring you home to their mother.

They say that after a while the feeling of separateness from the rest of the world doesn't end. They say you know when you got to quit because you feel 100 percent disconnected, 100 percent under water.

They say you're thirsty all the time and everything in your body is wet and your teeth and bones hurt and the fluid in your throat is blood.

That's why I know I've got to be as mentally strong as the devil and all his demons and get the fuck out when the time arrives, before the separateness is complete, before I go for a bath.

This game is the biggest human test of them all. It's heavy-weight battles over and over and your opponent, that stuff in the glass, he never gets any weaker.

This game is no indulgence, it's endurance.

I get a text message just as I'm slipping off to sleep in my easy Spanish hotel, just after the clock hits Mallorca midnight.

Number unknown. It's a pain in the arse. I'd been drifting away nicely.

The text says, 'You are going to die.'

I'm like, 'Aye, right.'

Chapter Five

Slept well.

Woke up ready to win the Bullfight.

First slash of the day and it's a confident start moving into full flow, into slow taper-off, to a couple of drops, to clear. You love a normal piss when your insides are your living, to know the engine is still doing the basics okay.

I take an early, easy run along the shore near where the ugly wedding cake cruise ships rub in and out of town.

One bloke recognises me, some guy alone. He points me out, open-mouthed, trying to remember my name. I reckon he's hotel bound after a long night. He points, then bends over and puts his wiggling index fingers on his head, bull-style.

I wave and he gives me the thumbs up. He starts laughing hard, staggering backwards. He's a hoot, whoever he is. Blocked, and likely soon blocked again.

That gives me a lift. Seeing that fella and getting a good night's sleep all have me thinking, 'You know, there's something beautiful about this rented-out town.'

It's seven in the morning and the big rich sun is promising to bring out lots of life today. Some guys are setting up fresh fruit stalls and talking loud, fast, happy Spanish. Some wrinkly, skinny woman with orange hair walks a dog that is – I swear – wearing sunglasses.

I remember I need a fresh pair, something quality to beat the rays on a long day. And I'm going to need some thick sun cream or I'll get fucking incinerated.

This day is going to be hot and great.

I meet Ratface for breakfast and we talk strategy. I say I need thick sun cream, factor multiple massive. I say I need sharp new sunglasses too but that I'll buy my own. He'd only buy some cheap fake shit that'd leave me blind.

'Cheap sunglasses are worse than no sunglasses,' I say, sipping apple juice. 'Your eyes think they're in the shade but they're getting fried like mushrooms in a wok. You need the UV thing and the cheap ones don't have it in the way . . .'

He goes, 'Jesus, Baker, shut up – what the fuck?'

We have a silence.

He's about to say something.

I say, 'There's a dog with sunglasses in this town. I swear, a dog with shades on its wee short face, dandering about with some oul doll.'

He says, 'I don't give a damn shit about that damn dog and neither should you, you freaking ass. Did you get a freaky text message?'

'When?'

'When do you think? Fucking twenty years ago, you crank . . .'

'I got one last night.'

'That's what I meant, Baker. Like, recently.'

'Yeah. Last night.'

'Saying?'

'*You're going to die*, or some shite.'

'Same, man. The same here, man. You get a number?'

'Number unknown.'

'Same, man. How can you even do that? Is it an app?'

I don't care.

He looks around, lands his eyes on innocent people getting breakfast, darts between them, darts at them. Our table for two feels all weird really fast.

'Fuck it,' I say. 'Who knows, who cares?'

'Yeah, fuck it,' he looks back, 'now listen . . .'

He starts, the advice, the phrases, the coaching. He tells me to pace everything during play and say as little as possible. He says to start as the quiet man, play up to the stereotype of the nervous rank outsider, let the longer-served pros nibble at me then bite back when they're nibbled out.

My game is best when it's long, more marathon than sprint, he tells me. He says to ingest the plan, to live the plan, respect the plan, stick with the plan. He says diversions are deadly, that my mind will start to manipulate. He says goals are glory, that victory is straight ahead.

He says, 'Goat Britches and that asshole Utility Nethercott are going to start hard, mark my words. Screw them. Let them do what they like.

'Don't fall for no damn peer pressure. Those guys are going to drink hard, like a team, going to try to make you do the same. I know their play.

'They'll laugh it up at guys like you, coax you into working faster than you can handle, make you feel like you're not doing enough to impress on your big break at the Bullfight. They want to make you feel weak out there.

'Don't do it, man. Drink to your own rules. Stay cool, play long, climb the ladders, step at a time, match for match.

'That way, when we get deep into the race, I know you'll sink them. They'll be too busy trying to sink each other's sorry asses to even notice when you start leaving them in the ditch.'

'Right,' I say. 'What'd you do last night?'

'I met everyone I needed to meet,' he says. 'I drank with some of the managers, picked up some shit about what's what. You heard of the Okay Apple?'

'Yeah. Guy called Lewis. Australian.'

'Yeah. No. Kiwi. New Zealand. He's a bastard. Watch him. He's been watching you. I figure he sees you as able to take this whole thing and he's going to sit with you, probably play as you do, shadow you, freak you. He's on you, dude. Don't ask me how I know.'

'How do you know?'

'His wife was on her phone to someone back home. She knows the game but doesn't know how to hold her liquor. Started saying cos you're twenty-seven and new that you know zip and don't have a hope.'

That's typical among the experts on this game, not the experts in it. They get drunk, loose-lipped. Ratface always had a thing for mingling with the roadies and groupies. He wasn't the only manager to do it.

Sometimes I wonder if people get him to hear things on purpose.

I say, 'She could have known you were standing there, listening in. It means nothing anyway. It's probably tru—'

'It ain't true. And who gives a fuck, Baker. He'll be watching you either way because he'll know about it, about that call, about what she's been talking about.

'You got to see beyond the 2D, man. You got to switch that dumb Irish brain on. I get thinking you're about sixty percent fucking brainless sometimes.'

He goes, 'Smarten up, man up, fuck up, shut up and listen up. Okay Apple will be wanting to know what you do no matter what. Fact is, *ergo facto* amigo, you're in his sights for a reason and I'm thinking there can only be one reason for that reason. You watch him. Watch everyone. Eyes open, open, open, all the time.

'We'll talk after Base about your conversation and about your eye contact game. Just keep mousey until then.'

Ratface suddenly starts pointing at me, jabbing from the elbow with every line. It's a thing he does.

'Speak only when necessary. Keep your eyes open. Don't laugh. Don't piss. Don't stare. Belch hard. Fart hard, never hold it in. Don't smile. Don't spill. And don't, above all, fucking jesus. I know you won't jesus.

'Keep your head up, hands steady, feet apart and drink those suckers, lead and dominate. Commit, down, clear, repeat. Focus on the goal, always the goal. Disdain the obstacles, your only interest is the goal. Got me?'

'Gotcha.'

'Good.' He takes his arm away, his bony little Rolex carrier, his veiny little cash grabber. 'We got a 12.30 photocall and you're in it. Wear the pink T-shirt and white cap. And don't shave. This is going to look like you care just enough to wear clean clothes, but not enough to groom.'

He says, 'Besides, you're a man, M-A-N. Tough and mean as dick muscle and rising to the occasion. Alpha it up, okay? Control your environment, got it?'

I say, 'Got it.'

'And most of all relax. Be the relax. Own the relax. So do some breathing exercises, okay tiger?'

'Yeah.'

'Okay beast?'

'Aye, yeah.'

'Good. Now drink that milk before it warms and I'll get you more toast. A lot more toast. Shitloads of toast. This is carbo city, right here, right now, and it's feasting time. You taken your Vit B?'

'Yeah.'

'How's your pissing?'

'Good flow.'

'Like it.'

He slaps me on the shoulder, alpha-style.

Chapter Six

I look like I've been playing paintball in this pink T-shirt. The *A$$tro* logo is yellow, a splash on the back with an arrow pointing down at my arse. Darby O'Kills have red and green bubbles floating up from my crotch on the front, kissing each other on the way up. The bubbles say 'Screw loose at Darby O'Kills' on my chest.

I look like a cartoon, a toy shop, a pervert.

I have to accept this crap. That's what a pro does. He accepts his fill of shite and alcohol and tries to keep a clear head. The sponsors paid my way, I have to pay them back.

I know they're still hesitating about me, about my longevity. You can never tell with a sinker, if he will break or die or run away or find a god or go to some waiting reporter and tell him the sport is evil.

So I reckon if I win, or at least play well, if I at least look like I have a good, hard career dead ahead of me, then I can probably talk about the kissing bubbles situation.

For now, I have to prove myself.

I push on the new shades and I'm the Reactor.

I meet the other fifteen fat, fashion-free wankers at the photocall, all of them walking around shoulders-first and insulting each other's mothers and wives and accusing everyone else of being gay and not being able to piss right.

Some of them want to know who I am and then say they've never heard of me when I don't tell them. I know from Ratface there's always an interest in the sixteenth seat, there's always a status goes with it. Everyone here knows exactly who I am.

I keep in mind how they think I'm dangerous, that they know I'm the university dropout, that they know I'm the half-baked failed solicitor who broke up his life to jump head first into this sport.

I tell myself they're assuming I'm the ginger Paddy who's going slowly, madly wild, the man who's left himself nothing but this, who's ready to get somewhere and take no prisoners on the way. I tell myself the ambition is ripping through me.

To be honest, I've so much Factor 50 on that I look like I've just climbed out of a box of lard but I don't let it bother me. I try not to picture what the others see. I focus on what's inside, on my affirmations, my little sinker prayers.

We sit around in arm wrestle poses and raised glass poses and *am-gonna-put-you-in-a-coma* poses as people take pictures. Gorgeous girls in black and red pout beside us for a while, sticking glasses and asses out as the shots are taken.

The mayor mingles in for more snaps, gets us holding up sangria and shouting *olé!* I can tell he's crazy about all this shite, his dark round face bursting into smile after smile when he feels viewfinders catch him.

He says he's sorry he hadn't met me the night before, that he liked to have a drink with all the Bullfighters and toast them with his heart and wish them the luck they deserve.

I ask him did he have a good time and he says he'd too much

sangria and I say, 'Sure why not?' and he nods deeply like I'm wise.

We walk to the big, round, wooden table in the main square, Placa Major, with people snapping and tweeting us and cheering all over the place. It's penned off, like a bullring, and hundreds of the sun-burning, big-hatted, pissed, shouting fans are already on stacked benches all around, some just ten feet from our seats.

There's one tented and guarded corridor leading off to the bogs and the medics. There's a big screen to one side so they can see our faces when we go in the back and piss.

Behind each stool we have our own señorita Servers, each with a big red and black chillbox parked right beside her. As ever, they're amazing. That frosty mist rolling over the clean, dark legs, that Spanish hair sucked back and shining, those air-tight red tees and black shoehorned shorts . . . the Bullfight never fails to sparkle.

Aye, the testosterone is already pumping, already trickling into our thick veins, ready to mix with whatever wham wine follows. These girls have a job to do and they're doing it good and hard before a beer is even pulled.

They tell you pro drinking is advanced imbibing, the oral Olympics, that it puts class in glass, that it's consumption for bar stars.

And for all that you need imaginative locations, arrangements, management and, like we have here, a simply superior selection of flesh and fandango.

The simple promise of possible flirtation is enough and it is essential. It's part of the balance, it helps stop this massively ugly, incestuous thing crumbling, it lifts a sinker's heavy, dripping heart.

I sip dashes of water as the head judge steps in saying he's Alberto from Pollensa. He rails through the rules in Spanish and English and no one but sinkers listen. We need him to know there's no tricks, no surprises, no little unseen cultural mismatches that might have got slotted into this lazily regulated battle. We need to see if we need to take a collective stand against something right away.

He calls in his two cronies. The three of them will be watching everything, taking the scores. Alberto jokes that by Fishermen – that's stage five – he'd be able to do it on his own, that more than half of us will be out anyway.

I think he's joking, but I don't know.

He says it'll be a hard fight, a true unashamed, proud Bullfight for the times we live in, that it will show the world that skill and courage and big balls do not belong to any section, any opinion, any philosophy, any sport.

He says he expects blood will be drawn, if only in the metaphorical sense. At least, that's what he might have said.

Ladies and gentlemen, your Bullfighters:

1. Howard 'Nine Hearts' Hazard (35yrs, 6'6") – Israel
2. Stephen 'Goat Britches' Ragner (33yrs, 6'1") – USA
3. Turna 'Scarf Arse' Follonini (30yrs, 6'2") – USA
4. K. P. 'Mad September' Jontel (29yrs, 6'4") – Kenya
5. George 'Street Sign' Ng (33yrs, 6'0") – China
6. Kipo 'Barbell Dong' Ini (38yrs, 5'11") – Australia
7. Jim 'Fireking' Henry (34yrs, 6'3") – England
8. Charlie 'Skull Dust' Hutchinson (32yrs, 6'0") – Scotland
9. Marcus 'The Okay Apple' Lewis (37yrs, 6'3") – New Zealand
10. Tris 'Bad Buck' Chauvrie (36yrs, 6'4") – France
11. Bosco 'Utility' Nethercott (35yrs, 6'1") – Canada

12. Raka 'Call It' Pallater (40yrs, 6'4") – Hungary
13. Yohan 'Tsetse Fly' Lambrecht (30yrs, 6'2") – USA
14. Brendy 'the Olive' Morrison (36yrs, 6'2") – Ireland
15. Leo 'Right Cyclops' Ozols (37yrs, 6'4") – Latvia
16. Baker 'the Reactor' Forley (27yrs, 5'11") – Ireland

Nine long rounds, the standard twelve minutes between. Standard 12oz glasses, standard volumes, standard debate and distraction encouraged in Base and Ludwig II – stages one and two – and demanded in the rest.

Minimal extra single points are always available for relevant and timely put-downs, self-ups or plain old great wordage in the heat of battle.

The judges decide what's worth what based on a side set of utterly fucked-up principles built up over hundreds of years and that are implemented in completely different ways in every country.

Stage one is Base, six beers, pacey but easy. It's not a race, just a warm-up, just a sizer, a scene-setter, a round for watching, feeling, gaming, for letting the punters get an early chance to do some bullshitting about prospects and odds. It's always beer, always a local brew or thereabouts. Every country in the world has a local beer, even the ones that don't.

We start with Estrella Damm, a 5.5 Catalan pilsner, glasses so chilled they're fighting the sun. Maybe it's because of the heat of that big sun but I have to admit it looks pretty good; good body, good settling weight for a starter beer.

The words 'good settling weight' roll around the table, meaning nothing, as sinkers clink and formally say 'cheers' in a language of their choice as the countdown starts at 'ten.'

It's all nods and well-wishing among us battlers as the fans shout it, '. . . nine . . . eight . . . seven . . .'

It's all sneers and hard stares around the table as they go, '. . . five . . . four . . . three . . .'

And it's nasty old 'now it's war' as the noise hits '. . . ZEROOO!'

The crowd bounces, beers high, roaring throats out, as the first sinker carries the first glass above the start pad and commits to hitting that first drink.

And, as a matter of fact, that sinker is me.

I say to myself, 'Keep 'er lit, Baker.'

'Hey Reactor,' some guy says. It was that Goat guy from America. He looks burned out, eyes like they've been open underwater, nose like some kind of floatation device. He's wearing a huge hat, a once-living kid goat now stuffed and running sideways atop his head.

'What's that, Goat brain?' I look away from him, a head turn can be as strong as a stare, so it can.

'Hey Reactor man.'

'Aye, Goaty fanny.'

'I heard they call you jesus.'

'I heard they call you Mary.'

'Yeah,' he says, drinking. 'I hear your mother's a whore.'

'Ah really? Is that your opening crack at me? Hilarious. Well your whore is your mother, ya prick. Ya fucking shambles.'

A fella two guys away laughs, a guy called the Olive, guy from Cork I've never spoken with. I know little about him even though he's an Irish sinker. Ears like car doors, a long beard pulled into a sharp point, a green cork on the end.

Ratface reckons this guy hasn't a chance, says he heard his wife died, heard his talking game has gone to fuck. Says to ignore.

I don't look at him. Why is he laughing at my lines? I'm not going to be laughing at his.

We are playing this fucking game now.

Fit your own mask first.

One guy has some kind of robotic croissant hanging from his shirt pocket and every few minutes it lights up and says 'Bad Buck will fuck you up' in a French accent.

One guy called Call It has a magnet through his nose, says it means he doesn't have to hold beer cans when he's drinking from them.

One guy called Mad September has pure white contacts and earrings made from miniature bottles of vodka.

Fat sinker called Fireking from Newcastle, England, goes, 'So you're the sixteenth seat wanker then?'

He's got a tattoo reading 'Fuck Off' on his upper arm, lines of cocaine and a £50 note badly inked on the other.

He wraps his hard hand around the beer, thick fingers showing what he thinks of my neck.

'That's right fat hand,' I say. 'That's me.'

'The least favourite then, the guy who hasn't a hope?'

'Whatever you say, Geordie girl. Did you get those tats for a bet?'

'Yeah, I bet I'd see ginger pubes by lunchtime and I'm looking at some now.'

He points at my head.

I go, 'Aye. And Stevie Wonder did them for you by the looks of it.'

He goes, 'What's the difference between a ginger and a brick?'

I know this one.

I go, 'What time you taking the heart attack then, dick fingers? I'm giving it about five minutes.'

He laughs. Then some others laugh. I don't know what to make of it. I do poker face.

A guy walking with a TV camera turns at me. I don't want to be his focus so early. I don't want to be noticed so early.

I get beamed all over the fucking planet.

I look at the camera and say, 'Difference between a ginger and a brick? At least a brick gets laid, so it does.'

I think how this is suddenly insane, that I'm suddenly in show-biz now.

Fireking says, 'I'll see you at the end of Ludwig and say "boo", just when they're taking you to hospital – if they can pick you up with all the fucking sun cream you've on, you Irish prick.'

I say, 'Cream? Nah, it's your oul wife's fanny batter.'

He says, 'So it's no wonder you look like a pussy.'

Others laugh.

I say, 'Aye . . .' drinking.

He says, 'You all done, pussy? No more for me? I'll kick your bloody head off your shoulders as soon as I'm done here, pussy Paddy.'

I say, 'Sounds scary, dildo digits. You're very scary, in your own way. Scary as a . . . custard bullet.'

He says, laughing, 'Custard bullet? Next time, say something with meaning.' And he laughs more and drinks.

I say, 'Fuck off you English cunt or I'll ram this glass through your face.'

Much laughter.

One steroid-blasted finger, flipped in my direction.

Attention turns to the Chinese guy, I'm glad to say. He gets some shit about squinting in the sun, some shit about Bruce Lee. The Chinese guy tells the guy his next drink will be his own blood.

I'm chilling and telling myself I'd had some cool, confident Attack and Engage. I'm not going to be too hard on me.

More sinkers get dragged into some hot wordage, maybe for show, maybe because they were too prickly in that fearsome mid-day sun, maybe because of a hundred reasons.

Four easy beers in and I'm sizzling like an onion in a pan, but the first man to request shade via one of the available umbrellas is going to get destroyed by these macho morons, by my fellow glass assholes.

I soak it up and get chatting with a giant, quiet Israeli across the table called Nine Hearts. Big eyes, big head, two chins.

Guy looks like something out of a fairytale, hair all spiked up, some kind of glitter on it, a black moustache like Hercule Poirot. He's rocking some kind of baby blue onesie, some kind of show with no arms, a picture of an old woman on the chest pocket.

A steady drinker, quiet sinker, leaks little.

'Decent name,' I say. 'Just saying, not fighting. Decent name, catchy. Not the worst.'

'Nine Hearts?' he says. 'Yeah, go and do some public suicide.'

'Is it based on anything, big head . . . or sparkly head?'

'Nine Hearts? Don't know. Yours, Reacting man?'

'No. Yet to find anyone who has one that makes sense.'

'What's that piss-yellow hat say – I Heart Derry Very Much? That a person or a place?'

'It's a state of mind, Nine Hearts.'

'Right. Must be an Irish thing, like drinking liquid shit and molesting children.'

'That's right,' I say. 'Not like an Israeli thing, all talking to walls and cutting your cock.'

'You're clearly a historical scholar,' he says, 'and I think the only one who ever gave a blowie to a stray cat.'

'Yep, I did. Now go stick an international conflict up your Israeli arse.'

Meh . . .

. . . a slim, toned arm rushes my empty glass from my start pad to my done pad, slaps another down an inch from my hand . . . it's movement so pure it makes me want to stop everything, tell everyone I hate them, and lick her fingers all day . . .

It's important never to get civil for long with these guys. You have to maintain an air of menace, of being a fucker, to show you're still in the game, to try to keep yourself simmering.

It's good to show you're ready to tear their family apart, their religion, their look, their skin. Nothing in the world is off limits when two guys are talking in this game, and that's part of why so many people despise it, why they love it.

In among all these people is no place for friends, for bonding, for finding anyone to trust because no one will help you out. Things get brutal out here among the industrial drinkers. The body can get hurt as sentiment hits. Everything can pile up so heavy and jagged that it can start slicing you open no matter what armour you packed in your belly or your brain.

When you get tolerance, when you realise your senses are dulling some more, it can start to feel important and front line and brilliant to be part of a mad, rebel, infuriating, rolling catastrophe like this.

A good worder, a worder who winds up and offends, can make good points on top of what he gets for his drinking, or at least take the title for the best worder in the match. It's not just about head-on collisions, it's about tactics too.

One guy might want to hit me with some hard verbals after three hours of maniac drinking and we might get all fired up and ready to throw some glass.

Then – example – I might belt him with something like, say:

'There's eleven sea shells on the moon. It's crazy. Sea shells, up there.' And point, point right up at where the big moon lives.

If you're lucky, he'll be drunk and angry enough to miss the point, to work out what the hell just happened.

He'll snarl and think of something and find himself saying, 'What you say?'

'On the moon. Pure madness.' I would point again, right up at the moon.

So the guy, langered off his fucking cerebellum, would look up. He'll be looking for the moon, lost with the moon, his train of thought all scrambled, all unable to find the train, unable to find the fucking station.

'And,' I would say, 'a small shovel too. A shovel. With a handle. Just think about that for a second. I mean, on the moon. Just lying there, ditched by an astronaut. The sea shells are a mystery though. So you think the moon and the sun are the same thing? What did they tell you in school?'

He'll be all, 'What the fuck . . . don't play the shit . . . ?' He'll be pulling himself back, trying to remember some affirmations. And a voice in his head will be going, 'What's that now . . . where was I . . . the moon? Shovel? Shells?'

And he was so fired up and so fluently interrupted he is on a one-way journey to adrenaline dump. And I promise you, that's a killer for a pro drinker. It makes the blood too rich too fast. It reshapes the stomach, wrecks all your appetites. It can bowl you off balance, write-off your game, shut down all your power.

Done sweetly, I've seen it end games so fast it almost ends careers. It's all about tactics. Get it right, the fans roar. Get it wrong, you're a total, stupid bastard of the highest order and you will be torn apart too hard for too long, and always for longer than you can take.

This rich Arab guy and his woman took two VIP seats up front in Base, just in the periphery of my left eye. I remember someone, somewhere had been talking about him, about some guy being soaked in oil, about him being the sport's wealthiest fan, about him never missing a big match.

He's what they call a Sheikh, an older man, a wise man. His clothes are white, clean as snow, thick, soft, full of brightness, never near oil, all royal style, head to toe. And the way he's sitting there, some wee fella in a suit standing behind him waving a fan at his face – aye, rich as a bank.

Next door, the big chair beside, is the woman. She's rolling in it too, but less jolly, less fat, less into watching a bunch of potbellied soaks retain liquid and dilute their brains out. She's the money shot, the sexy thief stealing that little show among horny fans. She's dressed black from head to toe, thin, strong, clean clothes.

They look like they smell lovely.

The TV camera fawns as they sit there, watching them watching. She's a chess piece queen on that high-backed throne, all wanted, all precious, all moves.

Queen? Sister? Wife? Daughter?

It hits you when you see a doll like that and you're spending your day with the sclerosis squad, with a bunch of guys who look like they should be helping the cops with enquiries. It's a tin of empty that hits you in the belly and holds itself there.

. . . and a flash of flesh, of quality skin, and a little gust of scented wind falls and dies on the side of my face . . .

I drink and I think how people are saying that's the life, that I've got a camel-toe tapas all around me, that I'm making fans and friends under the big sun, how I can hear cheering, how I've just been handed a beer so cold it could crack my bones by a girl so hot her shadow could boil balls in the bag.

They'll be thinking, 'You're such a dick, losing focus, sitting there thinking about the untouchable doll wrapped up in the carpet.'

And they'd be right, so right.

She has a bottle of soft, pure water in her hand. She's looking at us like we are taking a mass shite in her infinity pool, like she wishes all the beer would just wash us away.

I need to sort myself out, get with the programme, think of the way I should think . . .

This sport is bad and bonkers but you could be digging roads, you could be flogging phones. There's tits and drunks and fights and cash and whiskey and tension and bets on which fat bastard might be dead in a day.

I think sometimes that I've just got to wise up more, I've got to genuinely relish my stay in this one last place where you just cannot be correct, where you must mis-conform, where you just have to reverse everything you've learned in order to be one of the great guys.

What's not to love, you bollocks?

And I flash a smile at everyone.

A Latvian guy says something to me and I think, 'This is the stuff of legends.

'Didn't some doctor tell me point four percent blood alcohol is close to lethal? Didn't the pro-drink specialist tell me he's seen point sevens among us who have lived? Don't you know, Baker, you're re-emerging in this life as some kind of fucked-up athlete, some kind of biological star?

'Keep 'er lit, my man.'

We live on the edge, looking out over everything everyone else has their back turned to. We see the world different, the other way round, inside out.

You say weak, we say strong. You say fear, we say fearless. You say disease, we say game. We don't get in and out of the office fast, we get the office in and out of us fast.

You see when our working day is over?

You have no idea.

You see when these fights end?

We all get up and do what we can to carry ourselves backstage, away from the cameras, from the fans, from the world.

We go in there and we all call on jesus.

Jesus is lord.

He appears and saves our sorry souls.

Between the aching bladders and pissing and puking and shouting and fighting and laughing and kicking and belching and falling and threatening and farting and shitting and grabbing some guy's face and singing and gasping, it's like the devil's throwing Halloween.

You have never in your life seen anything like backstage at the end of a pro-drinking competition.

It can feel like the best place in the world to a fool like me.

Chapter Seven

After a hard tequila clocking in Fishermen, stage five, we're down to twelve men.

I am on my side, I am whistling through this day.

No one is trying to make jokes now.

No one is underestimating me.

We have beaten halfway through, all battling ourselves now to maintain, all trying to keep bullshitting as nice and clear as the other guy.

We're doing it between belches.

We're letting rip between letting rip.

If I can hold this situation, I do believe victory is straight ahead.

The Arab beauty is still watching. She's witnessed us wee pawns do our grog-to-urine trick for a long time now, and I look at my flashing glass and start to wonder what she's thinking.

We're a strange site to someone who comes from a place where no one is supposed to drink at all.

I come back from the bogs moments before Father Geoff, stage six.

I raise a hand and say 'Hi' to her as I pass.

It hits me how she's just watched me, those Cleopatra eyes, pissing about ten pints into a big clear, plastic bog.

Those priceless eyes, all heavy mascara and shiny, black-shad-owed edges. I see jet black and pure white flick as she throws them at me then whips them away. She isn't totally interested in the fact that I've stopped now, maybe four feet from her, that I am waving my hand.

Some girls are shouting for me, yelling, 'Reactor!' and 'Baker baby!'

I could get my oats after all this.

I could be peeling some cool holiday hardly knickers off hot skin after this.

A puke and a lie down and ten bits of toast and a shag.

I feel like doing a little dance for the doll. I feel like seeing if this Arab fineness will offer a smile as the drunk girls whoop.

I shake my shoulders, tilting side to side, standing in front of the impossible.

It's funny.

It is funny, isn't it?

Yeah.

I just realised how fucking horny I am.

My glass grabber is still raised in her favour, my legs are locked all tight in case they rubber, but I plan to get them moving in a sec. I take my hat off and wave it around a little.

Is Derry a person or a place? That's what that Israeli guy had asked.

You know, that's a deep question when you're blocked.

I say, 'A deep question, I think you'll find . . .'

And I do a little bow.

Her hair is covered, but her face is all show, all tight in the richness of that black headscarf, like her nose, eyes, skin had pushed through a wall of pure oil, like little pools of black gold had collected in the contours before those lids flashed open.

I say, 'Class, class, classy, class.'

I take off my shades and give another wee bow.

I'm really into good faces.

I can accept bad issues if they're attached to a good face.

And, Jesus, I love that oval one, that yellow, white, brown, coffee, tea, olive, whatever-it-is face. I want to kiss it and talk to it and take it to dinner.

There's cheering and she looks at me. I can hear Ratface somewhere, calling my name.

'Hey, Christ sakes, Baker . . .'

He can wait.

I'm having a break here, the next stage hasn't started.

I know what she's thinking. She's thinking I'm a bad day, a horrible night, all balancing there red and soggy in the heat, all fart and gorged-up, all grin and beer and piss and collapse right in front of her, all the last things she wants in her life rolled into one wet dribbling sack.

Her look says all that. I knew she was perceptive, correct, disgusted, and I completely understood. I reckon now I want to tell her she's right, but in a weird way she's wrong at the same time.

Make sense?

She's right to disdain. She's no fan of mine, no fan of pro drinking, and why should she be?

Right under that mad sun's big witness, she's so sharp and different and right and wrong.

I hear him, 'Hey Baker . . . Chrissakes . . .'

Whatevs.

This woman is definitely very wrong about me.

I feel like my head is being embraced by fire.

I wink, or I think I wink. I do something with my face, with my eye area.

BELT.

Some guy punches me in the stomach. It's a small, hard, fast cannonball right into the back of the gut, right to the spine.

I U-bend. I hit the deck like a shot horse. I hit the deck with my arse, then my head, then with everything I have, my hands too pissed to save me.

The world spins, washing machine cycle: a flash of the sky, a flash of a hundred legs, of a glass, a grin.

The hot stew inside fills my throat like a sewage pipe.

And now, for the first time in my short pro career, the warm comforting spirit of the Verb Jesus is appearing – everywhere.

Remember to roll, no matter what. Remember to roll.

I get helped as I try to turn onto my side, my front, to see some solid ground. Some guys lift me a little, to let it all fall out. I'm heavier than I ever felt. It's like something's landed on me, like gravity's stacking, multiplying on top of me.

I'm on my hands, arms aching, and choking and pouring it again, breathing in through whatever hole in my face I can.

And I'm right there by the dainty doll feet of that sweet honey-coloured girl in the black.

A camera is on me. A hundred cameras are on me. A lot of pictures get taken.

I am, in seconds, viral.

I am, right now, the world's biggest fucking mess.

I hear shouting and laughing and screaming, all anger and joy.

And her shiny blue, sparklingly decorated toes, with their perfect tiny butterflies dancing along her perfect skin, tense together, recoil and retract. Her little feet shrink and slip silently away from the periphery, just away from the edge of my rippling puddle.

My head says, '*Fit your own mask first.*'

On my knees now, sucking in air, eyes closing. But my belly wants to go again, has more to eject. I drop my head, lean forward, find out too late I forgot my arms, find I'm no longer supported by anyone.

I slap face first onto the ground, a hot splash of me into mine.

Chapter Eight

I don't have lasers that can shoot out my eyes and cut off hand-cuffs.

I can't lift much more than you and I don't have a gun that's a golf club.

I don't rescue babies, jump off the tops of trains or whatever.

I can't claim to have any of that hero crap. I got none, nada.

But I can drink perfectly, I can use alcohol repeatedly, way much more so than you, and I can make my way home afterwards.

Ask in any bar anywhere, and someone there will admire that extraordinary quality of mine. They would shake my hand if they could. They would buy me a drink if they could.

It's all written down in my constitution, article one: I can drink like a legend. Some people can paint, some can hold their breath, some can look like they are carved from marble.

I can drink like a nation.

I can drink like it's going out of fashion.

I can drink like there's no tomorrow.

But I have to stop if you punch me in the stomach.

Ratface is furious as a wasp. He's raging like a war. Not so much with the act of violence committed on me, more with everything and everyone he comes in contact with.

When I woke, he shouted at me. When I tried to speak back, he shouted. The hotel room phone rang and he answered it like the body on the other end was stone deaf and trying to kill him.

He'd already thrown stuff around the room like a madman. There was some chocolate stuck to the TV screen. Chocolate or shit.

'Right,' I say. 'Calm down, for fuck's sake.'

'Calm down? Are you INSANE?'

'Maybe.'

'I can't calm down. This whole thing has gone to hell in a dollar bucket. Hell's Bells! We're fucked, Baker. Congratulations on being the still-alive guy with the shortest pro-drinking career in history.'

'Nah,' I say. 'We'll be all right.'

'Nah?'

'Nah. You're just riled up, seeing red.'

'RILED UP! You're FUC—'

'OKAY,' I say. 'Jesus Christ, take it easy – you'll take a coronary if you're not careful.'

He stands looking at me, still as stone.

I smile for one second and his wee fists clench.

'So who hit me anyway?'

He turns around, looks out the window at the deep blue sea, turns back.

'You don't even know?' he says, quieter. 'You don't know? What do you know, Baker? Do you know anything?'

'I was too busy falling down to check who did it.'

'It was the fan guy, the guy waving the damn fan for the Sheikh. The Sheikh's bodyguard, in the suit. He hit you.'

'Right. I didn't see him coming.'

'Yeah, well he saw you and you were staring like a dribbling pervert at that chick, trying to wink your dumbass face at her, at the Sheikh's wife, you fucking glorious idiot.'

'She's his wife?'

'Yeah, his wife. The multibillionaire's wife. The big, powerful pro-drink fan's wife.'

'He's a lucky man. She's some bit of stuff to look at, eh? I mean I'd love—'

'The game, Baker. What the hell happened? You lost track because you liked a chick in the front row? Is that it? Is that how SHIT you are at focusing? Is that how much of a colossal douche bag you are?'

'Don't worry, we'll be all right. I think it was the heat or something, just made me feel all pissed too early or something. I was doing well though.'

I smile.

'You know your problem?' he says. 'You don't worry, Baker. Nowhere near enough. You need to worry more. Now is the time to worry. Never been a righter time to worry than right now. Worry like mad, a lot, as soon as you can.'

'So what happened with the game? Is it over?'

'Yeah. The Israeli giant shaded it. Howard Hazard.'

'Right. Nine Hearts? He's dead on.'

'Fuck you. I'll be in the bar.'

Ratface lets the door swing all the way so it bangs on his way out, but it's on a soft hinge and makes the kindest closing sound you ever heard. I know that will have annoyed him.

I sit in silence and try not to focus on my stupidity.

I try to take levity in the remains of the drunkenness, some delight in the clear fact that I had been gliding through the game.

I send my brain running around my body. There's no major headache or bellyache or anything much to talk of at all. I just feel dry, dehydrated. My stomach hurts, but no more so than say if I'd done a couple of crunches or Pilates or something.

I grab my phone. It shakes and squeaks and buzzes and toots out all these gone calls at me, all these messages and mentions and texts. I skim down and it's not good. I have suddenly got hated like a ferocious new disease. I take a peek at Twitter and I can't even tell you how famous I am, I have no way of measuring how big my name is.

One text slides in and doots as I sit there, my whole life in my hand.

It says number unknown.

It says, 'Shame will not kill you. But I will.'

I say, 'Aye, dead on.'

I drink water, scrub my teeth, take a shower and wash off the sun cream remnants. I get on some jeans and a white shirt. I'm looking at myself in the mirror, blotches of sun burn, patches of geisha white.

I smile at me. I make me laugh.

I drink water.

Fuck it.

Keep 'er lit.

And I'm ready to go face the world downstairs.

The door knocks.

I open and some small wide guy with a small square beard is standing there in a suit.

He pushes his hands together.

I say, 'How're you doing?'

He says, 'Yes. I come to apologise.'

'Right. What for?'

'For the hard hitting your stomach.'

'Oh right, Jesus – was it you? You the guy with the fan?'

'Yes. I'm sorry.'

I find myself reaching out, taking his tough little hand and giving it a good old shake like we're long-lost mates.

'It's okay,' I say. 'No problem at all. You know, it put me off my game a little but shit happens, like. My fault, to be honest. I was all slung with the booze and the temperature and all and lost my focus, you know?'

'I see but feel very bad,' he says. 'My job is to keep men feeling peculiar or sore when they take a shine to the Lady Crystal, the woman you were admiring at.'

'Yeah? Fuck. That's some job you have there.'

'Yes. It can be. She is, as they say, pictureness.'

'Yep.'

'Yes.'

'Well, no hard feelings.'

We shake hands again. Part of me is wondering why I'm being so gracious about all this. Maybe it's guilt for thinking what I'd thought about the Lady Crystal. Maybe the drink and the weather and the sleep had chilled me. Anyway, I'm enjoying a wee random sprinkle of happiness, of contentedness, and I don't want to spoil it.

'My name is Nap,' he says.

'Nap? Baker.' Some more handshaking.

'Yes. The Reactor.'

'Aye.'

'Sheikh Alam would invite you kindly for drinking at his house to say the most personal apology for my behaviour.'

'Really? Your boss? Wow. That's decent of him but I don't drink socially.'

'He knows that good fact. This is business. He told me to say this would not be social, but that it be business. He would talking business, put one good proposal to you also and he would be talking apologise.'

'Business?'

'Yes.'

'Hmm. Okay.'

'I bring the car here at 10pm, okay?'

'Yeah, sounds okay.'

'Thank you.'

'Thank you.'

We shake hands a little while more and then bow at each other. Nap walks away, backwards at first.

He doesn't look standard tough, but he is massively strong. His hands are solid, a fist like the big end of a small baseball bat. I reckon I may have the imprint of one of his knuckles on the inside of my spine.

I go down to the bar. Ratface is talking crap with one of the Americans' managers. They're both agreeing the sport is going downhill, that no one respects the talent anymore, that presidents never wish the US players well anymore.

Ratface had said the same crap a lot.

The guy shakes my hand.

'Sorry for what happened to you, Baker. You'd had great Campaign and Fishermen, steady and sharp. You were looking good. You were going to do all nine, no doubt.'

'Yeah, thanks. I'd been feeling good, you know. I think I could have done it.'

He says, 'You could have won. That heat's a damn killer though.'

'Yeah, well, I've survived to fight another day.'

I excuse sighing Ratface and take him to a wall. I tell him about the apology upstairs from Nap. I tell him I've been invited to the Sheikh's place for a drink, that the car will be here in half an hour.

'He said it wasn't social,' I say. 'Said it was going to be an apology and a business proposal. What do you think?'

'Don't know. Strangeness. That might just be his way of saying, you know, come to my place because I'm a big shot and I got a house in Mallorca and I'll just talk shit when you get here. Rich assholes do that stuff. I've done that stuff. It might be for real though.'

'Aye. So, I'm asking, do I go?'

'Of course you go, Baker. And so do I go.'

'The invite's just for me.'

'Fuck you. If there's going to be business talked, I have to be there. You don't know shit about business.'

'I don't know . . .'

'Screw you, I'm going. I can't let you go alone for legal reasons. And it wouldn't be right to leave you alone with that freaking fan-waving Oddjob dude anyway.'

I don't say how I think the Oddjob dude's a nice guy.

He says, 'Did you get a freaky text message?'

I go, 'I got millions of them. I'm the biggest tit on the planet right now.'

He nods. He looks around, he snarls, something unpleasant suddenly bubbling up inside.

He says, 'You know something, Baker.'

I say, 'What?'

He goes, 'I can rip a man's head off with my bare fucking hands if I need to.'

I say nothing, then I go, 'Dead on.'

Chapter Nine

The problem when you're a pro drinker is everyone wants to have a drink with you. Everyone buys you a drink everywhere you go. They're having a smoke at a pub door, see you walking down the street and they'll buy a shot for you, hold it out for you as you pass by.

The sport buys you all you can handle and then some guy buys you one more to sink with him, like he's doing you a favour.

I say, 'Cheers, no.'

They say, 'Stick it up your fucking arse then, cunt.'

Some low-rent drinks companies are at it too, sending out stuff and hoping for your endorsement, hoping you'll stand around posing with their shit in your hand, using their slosh as your private, pro-picked slosh of choice.

In no time I was getting six packs of gakky gassy beer and bottles of half-arsed Irish whiskey arriving at my miniscule north London flat. The first batch arrived about six hours after I was launched online as the Reactor, the new kid on the block, the big ginger hope from wee Derry.

It was only a few days later that I started to notice some dodgy-looking thirsty oul bastards had started hanging around outside, glancing up at my window, winking at me when I went out for a paper.

No prizes for guessing they'd found out a sinker had moved in.

I've left some of the oul shitty liquors outside the door since and it shifts faster than a dog on a beach. I've left some of the rest of the dung too   the beer mats and branded lights and pens and hats and flash drives and knickers and condoms – but there isn't as much interest.

Those guys think I'm the luckiest guy in the world.

Many people do.

They think we've all hit the jackpot just because our sinker bodies clot and blot and hold like nappies, that we are paid to consume, that consuming is joy. They won't listen but the fresh truth is the drinking is the bad part. The good part is being clean and sober, and that can be a world away sometimes.

You know, it can take weeks to feel normal again after training and competing, and you never have weeks to spare, you're never brave enough or free enough to let the tolerance wither.

The PDA are no help. They want the whole world to think pros are super lucky, that we've gifted lives, that we're the real all-time, true celebrities. They say sinkers are celebrities who get fatter not thinner, who laugh as they work, who have life by the balls.

But no one listens to that kind of bollocks anymore.

Now the PDA are hoping PDTV, the new online channel, will save the whole sport from oblivion. It's 24/7 telling the story of the glorious ancient history of competitive drinking, the amazing yarn of the sport of the bold and the brave, of the game of legal excess once played by playboys on silky beaches, by god-appointed kings in draughty castles, a game which once almost made it into the summer Olympics except the world champ at the time dropped dead during an interview.

Ships and daughters and farms and lives have been staked, won and lost over this sport. Years of bloodshed have started because of this sport.

If the pressure groups get their way, one day there will be a list of the dead somewhere, some volunteer victim memorial, and everyone, everywhere will be able to find some blood on it somewhere.

For now the PDA will talk only about living heroes, about rippling, expanding, heroic giants, about mind-blasting feats of absorption, of exquisite self-control that, they say, only the short-sighted and self-centred could want written out of the past.

They sit around like tobacco magnates in big, tired seventies' offices, stacked to the slates with alcohol, wondering how the hell they can get more people, more fans, more players, more games, more future.

They want to duck under and back through the trajectory of global thinking and drinking and carve out some genuine clout on social networks. They sit around saying how we are on the edge of an era of purer democracy, where everyone owns media, where popularity will be its own success undiluted by the most cynical, brutal, twisted, buckled, sick and nasty politics of them all, the rotten politics of health.

And, just so you know, they do a dirty little social media side-line in catching and pushing those few-second bits of footage of sinkers who've been drinking so hard they're fucking boneless, clueless and hopeless because it goes all over your laptop, whoever you are, and it gets you laughing.

They calculate that collective laughter can help drown out and wrongfoot scorn, pity and anger. Their marketing gurus say that's the way forward in a world where reality comes in short bursts, where it's about as much what you don't see as what you do, where punters want to focus on the real action but can't be arsed with the full picture.

They reckon they can get away with this for a while longer.

I hope so too, just so I can make a few quid and get out to fuck before I die.

Yeah, I know.

I'm *that* nice.

Part of me goes 'fuck society' and then part of me goes 'Baker, you're a wanker.'

But I've tried, so I have. I have tried.

There is actually fuck all else I can actually see through to the end, other than an absolute fuck of a drinking session.

So I'm thinking how she's called Crystal and is all slim and firm and soft all at the same time. How she has these narrow, coffee-bean eyes and high-quality skin with no colour I can name. How the hair could be ebony or red or chestnut, how I've only seen her face and gentle hands.

I'm thinking I haven't even seen the shape of her arse, not properly, but I can picture something that looks like a heart.

How I'd like to see that.

I'm wondering if I'll see her again.

Ratface insists on getting into the car with me, telling Nap it's either both of us or none of us. He touches my arse as I bend over a wee bit to get in.

Nap says it's all cool, that if he wants to come it's cool, that whatever is cool. He apologises again, just to get it on the record with a witness present.

Ratface makes a point of saying some horseshit about me still having to speak to my lawyer about it all. He tells Nap I still have to tell the full story of that punch in the gut to the press, that I haven't yet decided how I'm going to play it. He tells Nap all about what I'm thinking of doing, and in my head I'm thinking, for some pointless reason, about the state of my life.

I hear myself thinking how I've fucked up the one thing I had.

I hear myself saying how I only had it because I fucked up the bit before it.

I think how I've fucked up a lot.

My dad was a fine solicitor and a great swimmer, fit and smart and sharp. He did what he could for little people who needed minor miracles. I remember he worried all the time, that he used to pace around in the night, flicking through papers and taking phone calls and trying hard to say 'no'.

Turns out he did so much pro bono work for the sad cases of the world that the bad cases found out, that his own goodness got non-stop used against him.

I wanted to be like him once, to have that depth of value he had.

What in the name of fuck he'd be thinking now, I just don't know.

The Arab's house, hidden away on top of a hill, looks like something that's crash-landed from another planet. It's a misshaped palace of twinkling lights with a fountain on the sloping roof blasting thick jets of water high into the hot night.

We'd passed by two stoned-looking security guards at the enormous iron gate, passed huge black, thick trees, and then onto a bonkers narrow driveway that zig-zags sharply upwards towards that emerging mental chateau.

Nap's stressed as all hell as he navigates, headlights full burst, like he's doing one of those don't-touch-the-sides buzzer games.

I can only figure the head man doesn't like Mercedes S-Class tracks on his snooker table lawn, even though his entire house looks like it's halfway through being torn apart by Godzilla.

'Designed by Gaudí,' Nap says, his voice a little higher than it had been.

He's struggling to see enough of the driveway over the steering wheel, gasping a little in his tight shirt and tie as he checks all around him, clinging like his life depends on it. A stubborn little bead of sweat hangs bravely off the end of his wee girl's nose.

I say, 'Gaudí? Is that right? The house or the drive?'

'You stupid ass,' Ratface says, shaking his head at me.

'Both,' Nap says.

He leads us inside, a front door like the side of a house, and down a corridor like a church, smiling all the way, nodding at paintings on the wall. They look like more stuff from space, or like they were painted in space, or painted by someone who was spaced. They could be worth twenty quid or twenty million. I see Ratface fast looking at them all, fast at the bottom right-hand corners.

We go up in an elevator like an office and pace silently down another corridor, totally oak, and into a room like a high-class shopping street.

Straightaway I feel power everywhere and I see the big robed Arab striding over. He's got his hand out for shaking even though he's fifty feet away.

I hold out my hand, and stand here, waiting, and waiting.

Should I walk?

It doesn't feel like I should walk.

Nap smiles at me a couple of times as we wait. I smile once or twice. Then again. I smile several times.

The Sheikh stares full beam as he comes, but I avoid his eyes and smile again at Nap.

Nap smiles back. He's learning to do short ones.

Eventually the man arrives and we shake, a big, warm, soft, clean hand enveloping mine. He does the same to Ratface. And right away, so he could do it in front of his master, Nap starts apologising again.

'Thanks Nap,' I say. 'No more needed. You've apologised for all of Arabia by now.'

I do a smile.

Nap does one and looks at his boss.

The boss laughs, Ratface laughs and Nap and I look back at each other and we laugh too.

What the fuck, like.

In the coming fifteen minutes I'm offered every combination of alcoholic drink on earth and I refuse them all. Then I'm offered some re-combinations of those and I refuse again. The Japanese woman doing the offering speaks like I'm a lip-reader, her delicate face forming the words, rearranging the words, interchanging the words, with more slow clarity and allure than I had ever seen in any conversation in any language.

'Cranberry, banana and gin?'

'No.'

'So we also have cranberry, apricot and gin'

'No, honestly. I'm dead on, so I am.'

'No? Perhaps cranberry, banana, apricot and gin?'

'No. Nothing.'

'Sheikh Alam insists his friends drink alcohol with him, sir. So I must see if I can find something you like. Melon juice and vodka?'

It was great though. It was like one of those haircuts that sends tingles up the spine, one you don't want to end. One where you think, 'Cut away, right to the dome, I love how you are making me feel at this moment.'

I could have watched her all day, just saying words over and over again, the movement of her speaking was so graceful. If I was rich I'd hire her too, let her sit around saying any oul random shite and I'd just look and listen and tingle and ignore the world.

Eventually it seemed decent to agree to something, and for some reason I settled on a white wine with some kind of mint in it. Maybe I'd been hypnotised. Then someone took off my shoes and gave me a grape.

Ratface, his little ratty nose twitching at the cool, deep scent of cash, is entertaining Sheikh Alam with the kind of gusto a fella rarely sees.

And now it's big heartbeat time as Crystal comes into the room, her searing eyes framed in that perfect black. She smiles like she's dangerous, all lethal up close, a flash of something too good to be safe. Her skin glows with hydration.

It's absolutely not what I'm used to and I want it.

'Hi,' I say, standing up, tipping my green-tinged wine towards her. I almost can't stop myself saying 'You just made my eyes reboot' or some shite, but thankfully I just shade it.

'Hi,' she says, checking out Ratface's horrible profile. It always gets a second look. It'll be the worst thing she's seen today.

'So,' I say, 'the idea was for me to come here to get apologised to. But, to be honest, I should be saying sorry to you too.'

'For staring at me and screwing your face up and vomiting on my shoes?'

'Erm, yeah.'

She doesn't sound middle-eastern. Her voice is gravelly, but fast. An English accent, but with many influences.

'Don't worry, Mr Forley,' she says. 'When men are around it's sometimes easier to wear the full face, but I can never be bothered. Could you be bothered with that?'

'With a veil over my face?'

'Yes. Could you be bothered with it?'

'You mean, would I wear one?'

'Yes,' she says, sitting down, growing tired of me already. A whole new woman was beside her in a shot, bowing and dying to take a drinks order.

'Probably not,' I say, sitting. 'In fact – not. Maybe if I grew up with it I might. It's not really part of my culture.'

'Yes, true, evidently. Soda and lime.'

I steal a look at the Sheikh. I know he isn't crazy about male attention on Crystal. Little Ratface has him interested enough in whatever shite he's talking about.

'So,' I say, honing in, pushing a fast, clear, foul thought from my mind, 'where you from?'

'Nuneaton. Near Birmingham.'

'Just to check, that's Birmingham in England?'

'Yes, in England. Not Alabama.'

'It's just your accent . . .'

'What about it?'

'Nothing.'

'And you? From where?'

'Derry. You know, Northern Ireland?'

'Ah yes, your accent.'

'Aye.'

'I think I've heard of it.'

'Great. Top left. It's known for all sorts of shite, like. You know, the Siege, the Troubles, some old bishop or something, whatever.'

She goes, 'Right.'

'We've got like Josef Locke, Undertones, different ones, Dana. We've loads of stuff, you know?'

I don't know what I'm on about here.

'Right,' she says, actually looking about a foot above my head now. 'Fantastic.'

I say, 'I thought you were, you know, from Saudi Arabia or somewhere. Just my assumption based on . . . you know.'

I point at her, then upwards at the top of her head.

She watches.

I stop pointing.

She nods.

'Easy mistake,' she says.

I think for a moment, take a drink.

I say, 'I have cousins around Birmingham somewhere.'

I don't.

She says, 'Brilliant.'

She's almost looking at the ceiling now, maybe about to pray I go away.

'Aye, well. Your skin's a nice, full tone, if you don't mind me saying. Most English or Irish are white as damned chickens. I know I am anyway. The ginger Paddy skin thing, you know? I'm proud of it in one sense, like. You have to be, don't you? But it makes the sun laser the balls off me every time I go outside over here. I'd say that explains the thing earlier, being sick and all.'

I absolutely don't know what I'm talking about.

She must get this all the time, this 'where you from?' routine. I look at her neck and think how she's perfectly tanned, how there must be sun all around her all the time, how it is always there for her in the places she goes.

I think how her skin has a name and nationality of its own.

And everything falls silent.

I'd have to snap my fingers here to get her to look at me now, but it would be rude and Nap would kick the fuck out of me.

I suspect for a second how she may have award-winning breasts, ones that deserve a medal each, but I really better stop thinking it, try to take more control of what I'm saying.

For a while the only noise comes from a ceiling fan and the scratchy rattle of Ratface talking about alcoholic corrosion of the throat which, as it happens, is a serious problem in my line of work.

Ice collides and clicks as the soda and lime arrives. She is offered, and takes, a grape.

'I got bored with the whole thing back home,' she says, eating, radiant teeth. 'I got offered a modelling job in Dubai and then,' she nods towards the Sheikh, 'he came along and did a bit of a woo.'

'Right. Rich as Midas by the looks of it.'

She looks at me, shows those eyes, nods sincerely.

She says, 'Richer. No one even knows how rich, not even him.'

'Nice.'

'Fuck, yeah. It's even better than you'd think.'

'Nice.' I like her honesty. She suits money, it suits her. Maybe they deserve each other.

'We were at a huge party in Dubai last week,' she says, 'being looked after by four hundred staff. He got his assistant to tip every single one of them a hundred thousand euro.'

I don't know what to say. I try to do a quick sum, but quickly give up.

'Rich as dreams,' she says.

I'm finding this conversation very exciting, somehow very sexy.

I might seize the moment.

I'm usually the play-hard-to-get kind, the guy who waits, who expects it all to come along in the end and doesn't try too hard. But none of that has ever worked for me in any way, shape or form.

'So listen Crystal,' I sit forward, put my hands around my glass, look at her and smile twice. 'Can I ask you something?'

She looks at me coldly, that face sucking my eyes as she takes a drink, those ice cubes tick-tocking cleanly in her perfect glass.

I could look at her all day.

She says, 'Is it about god?'

'No. It's nothing to do with god.'

'Good. People always ask me about that, about religion.'

'Oh, right. Yeah, because of the . . .' I wave my right index finger around the outline of my own face, trying not to point at her again, '. . . thing.'

'Yeah.'

'Right. No. But I might actually ask you that.'

She had made me interested as soon as she said it. I don't know if she's a Muslim but I do know, for what it is worth, that she had said 'fuck'.

'What I was going to say was this,' I say. 'To be honest, I haven't got a whole lot . . .'

Ratface butts in, 'Hey, Baker.'

'Jesus, yeah.' I look to him, slowly. He's a shit in the caviar, a spit in the Champagne.

'Come here, man.'

'I'm sorry,' I say to her. 'Business.'

She smiles a classy, easy smile. 'I know.'

I stand, nod a bit and go over. That Sheikh is grinning like he's got fishhooks pulling at his mouth. Ratface is doing that look where he narrows his eyes, as if he's trying to read something far away, but isn't.

I get the feeling I'm about to learn something.

Chapter Ten

Ratface says guys who wave a fan in front of someone's face are called *punkawallahs*. I don't know how he knew that.

'How do you know that?'

'I know a lot of stuff,' he says, winking.

'So Nap's a *punkawallah*.'

'Evidently.'

'Great.'

'You think?'

'Could be worse.'

'Right.' Ratface shakes his head, laughs a little. 'You're freaking nuts, Baker.'

Ratface has about nine different opinions of me.

He has one unwavering opinion of my arse, which he has just touched.

We are taking the hotel stairs, bags in hands. The elevators are broken. A crowd of sinker fans got all high-spirited the night before, smashed the buttons. They'd already bashed up some rooms, wrecked the bar, kicked a piano around, some other stupid shite too. One or two of them got arrested. It made the news.

Ratface and I saw the tail end of it as Nap dropped us back from the Arab's house.

Where there's pro drinking, there's damage.

The press conference is in the function room by reception. They're usually only interested in the winners or the guys with the best words the day after this comp, but today I'm on the radar.

It wasn't the first time a sinker had been bowled over during a game and it wouldn't be the last, but it was the first time it had happened at the Bullfight, and the first time in a long time that it wasn't even a sinker who did the thumping.

I take a seat at the end of a long table. All sixteen of us are pulling up places, facing the world, all sucking on water and thick, cold air-con. Behind all those shades and low-down caps I can make out some washed-up, sweaty looking hounds. Nightmares are swirling through those beadies, swinging and swaying and boiling up like daylight monsters.

The Israeli guy Nine Hearts' cheeks have swollen out like a hamster – they call that Face Flood.

The Irish guy Olive's lips look like they'd been inflated with a bicycle pump and beaten with iron bars – they call that beauty secret the Bloot.

The Okay Apple is dripping like cheese in the desert and that Fireking dickhead is trembling like a helicopter.

'Hey Baker, Baker – Shelly Vinner, *EuroGame*. How're you feeling? That was one bad belly blow you got, right?'

'Yeah, and thanks. It was a misunderstanding. No malice in it. I'm sorry to have had to bow out so gracefully, so I am, but that's the way it went. Sure what can you do, like?'

Some laughter.

'Jack Melody, PDTV Online. It's a bad start to your pro game, right Baker?'

'Not the best. I'm not used to the heat and all, being from Derry and all. But that just makes me more determined.'

That would be Jack bastard Melody.

It would be Jack fucking Melody.

The hated Jack Melody.

There's a couple of chuckles at me from the bench, from those still connected enough to the world to know what's going on.

Melody presses the point with his supersize jackpot smile, 'What was the big misunderstanding? Something to do with who you were . . . let's say . . . looking at?'

'Was I looking at someone?'

I flash a small smile.

'Yeah Baker,' he says, raising half a top lip like Elvis. 'With your eyes on stalks and your mouth open.'

The room laughs.

Everyone points machines at me.

I smile.

I can hear Ratface kicking off somewhere behind, I can hear him moving into shot.

'Hey, Melody, you waffling moron,' he says, outraged. 'Baker Forley is a pro, best damn freshest damn pro on the circuit. What's your problem?'

'No problem, coach. Just wondering why a bodyguard punches a sinker during a comp. You'd know that if you had a clue about pro drinking.'

Mirth.

Phones tinkling.

Ratface, boiling, goes, 'Yeah, I do, you plastic-faced, surgically enhanced shitbag. And like the man says – misunderstanding.'

Raw laughter.

I shrug.

'That's what it was, Mr Melody,' I say. 'A misunderstanding. Shouldn't you be asking Nine Hearts about his game? Last I heard was he'd won this Bullfight.'

Melody chuckles.

Ratface half-shouts 'asshole'.

Nine Hearts looks up like he's just started taking a heart attack.

Ratface comes forward a little from the back, just to my side, his mouth puckered up like a sphincter.

He makes a slit-your-neck sign at Jack ball-breath Melody.

There's history there, bad stuff.

Do not ever talk to Ratface about Jack bastard Melody.

I never even got the opportunity to go home after that. Ratface had hoped he could factor in some time for the two of us to fly off for some R&R, but it didn't work out that way.

Sheikh Alam was too keen, too ready to enact his plan for us. He wasn't the kind of fella who heard the word 'no' very much.

I'd told him I'd do it. I said I'd come and drink with him at his crazy Gaudí mansion, but that I needed some time, a few days out.

Ratface said the same, that he'd play his part and advise and train Alam, but that he needed a few days back at his Florida beach house in Pittsburgh to sort his shit out.

The Sheikh had seemed pretty surprised by our answers. Nap had looked like he was going to melt right there on the floor of that big room when he heard us object.

'My friends,' Alam says then, 'I am leaving Palma in eighteen hours in my yacht. I am going to circle the bay, take in the view, move northwards at a leisurely pace and return to Palma the next morning.

'This is the fact, the fact of the tradition of my holiday time spent in Palma. I have to get some use of my ridiculous yacht.

'And you see, my friends, I can't change my mind once I have made it up. So come with me for my annual pointless yachting then come back to my house.

'Or do not do either.

'But, gentlemen, I ask respectfully, do not agree to spend time with me in my places and then change my rules.'

I felt like asking him who the hell he thought he was, but Ratface took over.

He did a lot of apologising and said we would work something out, make a few calls, chat to the sponsors back home, fix things up so they go the Sheikh's way.

Ratface told me later the sponsors wanted a meeting and how that this was his biggest worry. He'd had to put them off, he said they weren't happy.

But he'd got clever, called them back, told them this business with the Sheikh was opportunity, a chance to put us forward as a private pro team for Saudi billionaires, as a hand-picked sinker and coach at the height of their powers, despite the obvious.

If the Saudis were at it, he told them, it was at the cutting edge of fashion and would amount to superior placing for the brands. He said it would only mean another week or so on the island.

'In my business, Baker, I got so many things to balance all at the same time,' Ratface tells me. 'You just got to glug down alcohol and stay alive, I got to think.'

'Yeah, right,' I tell him. 'Aren't you supposed to make me feel good?'

'Yeah,' he says. 'That's another bullshit thing I have to do all the time.'

Sheikh Alam had been blunt about what he wanted from us, as if we had already agreed we would do what he asked before he asked it. The guy had been spoiled his whole life.

Still, he was rich as jazz so he got his way.

He told us he drank when he could, but that his family were the problem. He said he loved quality gins, whiskeys, wines, ports and beers, but that he had about 150 relatives living close by back in Saudi and every last one of them was seriously strict about the no-alcohol rule.

He said it was partly religious, partly cultural, but deadly serious among his family.

He told us, head shaking, 'I sometimes cannot shit in my private room in my private house without some fucking cousin I can't even name knocking on my most private door to ask me some detail about something.

'I have a bath and a fucking cousin is standing in my room when I get out and she is drinking a soda from my fridge and she wants to talk to me about writing or fashion or fucking money. I say get out of my life! Where could I even hide my beer? I am forty-five years old and richer than the bloody banks of Switzerland yet where can I have a bottle of hooch? Hardly possible, my friends, hardly possible.'

'Nightmare,' I say. And I meant it too.

'Yet I love to drink,' he says. 'I love to be around it. I love to watch people with it, to see them happy and drunk. I love to smell it and taste it and let it spin my head and sing and dance and sleep with my fill of drink. I love to be among alcohol and all the wonderful oily freeness that it means, the wonderful ethos that it brings.'

He stared at me then, for a while. He has a happy face, big, warm, clean, well-smiled, bearded, expertly shaved around the edges.

I say 'Great.' I shrug.

'I want to drink with you,' he says, pointing. 'I want to master it from you, my Irish friend. I want to be awash with it like you. I want to freely drink with you, to drink more and more like you.

'I go to all pro drink games in Europe and America and I am excited to see you come into the business, Mr Forley. I really was looking forward to seeing you at the Bullfight, to see your style, your business of drinking, your flow, your angles, to hear your exciting words, but of course it went tits up with the assistance of my overeager little friend Nap.

'So it makes me comfortable to know I can put all the staring at my wife's eyes and breasts to the one side and be your friend and say simply to you these words – I want to drink with the Reactor. And I want to drink like the Reactor. Do you understand?'

I say, 'Jesus. Fucking hell. I do.'

Ratface feels the same, but he had known all this ten minutes before.

'Come on my private yacht with my other new drink friend and Bullfight winner, the great Mr Nine Hearts, for just one night. We have servers on there, the Spanish servers from the Bullfight. They very discreet.

'One beautiful drinking night on my yacht. Then, my friends, our yachting is over and we relax in this house and drink and drink and eat and drink and you will teach me to drink and drink. You and you.'

Ratface had already assumed he was included. He didn't need to get pointed at by the big square finger, manicured to the furthest point manicuring can go.

'I learn from the best in my own house,' he said. 'And, gentle-men, as the Spanish say, *mi casa su casa*.'

The Sheikh stopped talking and Ratface scratched his nose and turned to me. I hadn't yet settled it all in my head, but I knew for sure he was keen.

Ratface says, 'Nice, yeah? Sun, yacht, Gaudí, Sheikh? There's freaking chefs at that house too. There's a freaking chef on the damn boat.'

I say, 'Pretty amazing, to be honest.'

'And if I may add, Baker, our good friend Sheikh Alam is offering a handsome fee for your time. For our time. Our expertise in this important business.'

'Oh yeah?'

'Yeah,' says Ratface. 'Oh hell, yeah. Mr Sheikh Alam here's offering,' and his voice dipped a little, 'a hundred thousand euro each to buy us both for the week.'

'Holy mother of hairy arsed Christmas.'

The only question I had left was 'Is Lady Crystal going to be there?' but I couldn't rightly ask it. I mean, I wanted to buck the guy's wife on the floor about twenty feet away. He didn't need to know that.

By the time I'd turned around to look her way, she'd gone. The maid was taking her glass and straightening up the cushion that had been graced by her dainty derriere.

Nap caught my eye, or I caught his, and he frowned energeti-cally. I looked back to the Sheikh.

I would have to leave all that stuff.

The yacht was setting sail at sundown the next day.

There is major money to be made and it could fix my whole life.

I will be, I do believe, very soon, I think you'll find, doing okay, thank you very much.

I'll be as rich as a waiter who served the Sheikh.

This man has a thing about a hundred thousand euro payments, I reckon.

But I'm not complaining.

That'll do nicely.

Nap meets us after the press conference to take us to the shops. We need to get some fresh clothes, some gear to do us for the extended stay. It's all going on the boss's credit card. I suddenly want to get some overpriced Ray-Bans, to start upgrading me immediately.

Nap's job is to look after us, to take us to lunch, to entertain us. And later he would be taking us to the yacht.

I keep thinking there's someone I should be ringing, someone I should be telling about this surprise adventure, but no one comes to mind. Perhaps I was with the right people, the only people who needed to know this radical detail about my journey through life.

Ratface tells Nap he wants to sort out the payment as fast as he can, just so everyone can relax on board, so everyone could give Sheikh Alam their full attention.

'Of course,' Nap says. 'I am instructed to take your bank account numberings and happily make initial happy transfer today. Come with me to the bank post eat. You can witness.'

'That was the "A" answer, my friend,' says Ratface, patting the guy on the shoulder. 'You are a true gentleman.'

'Hey,' I had to butt in, to mark Ratface's card. 'Your account?'

'Baker,' he says. 'Zip that greedy cakehole.'

Chapter Eleven

When someone asks what your favourite song of all time is, just say the first one that comes into your head.

It's a stupid question.

Anyone who really likes one song will really like some other song too. You don't fall in love with one song and stay away from loving others. What would be the point of that? You don't marry a song. Absolutist shite is always mad.

But people like to ask crap and talk crap and tell themselves it's not crap. They like to read magazines and see what someone's favourite word or colour or number or smell is. They're thinking it tells them something about the person but it tells you nothing about the person. The question is as total balls as the answer.

I just say, 'Whatever, anything.'

I just say the last song I heard, or just make one up. I don't give a flying fuck.

You can read my mind because I say I like blue or black or green?

You're insane.

I've been asked about my favourite drink, favourite memory, fave movie, actor, sinker, place, TV show, drink, country, whatever.

I have none.

I just say, 'Aye, best song of all time? "Rivers of Babylon", Boney M.'

Or I go, 'Best ever song? That old Irish ditty about the woman who kept a cow up her mary.'

Some reporter rang me up and said, 'We're doing profiles of Derry people in the news, so we are. What's your favourite song?'

I said, 'Let me see now, it's either "Waltzing Matilda" or Hammertime.'

He goes, 'Dead on. You like the Undertones or Van the Man or U2 or any Irish bands? You like Snow Patrol?'

And I go, 'No, they're all shit. Oh wait, my favourite is definitely that one by that chick-diddler Katy Perry, or maybe the one that fella with the bouffant sang in 2006. The Kate Bush 'Wuthering Heights' one is probably second. And that sixties' guy who had a sex change was pretty amazing.'

He goes, 'Dead on.'

Ratface asks shite like that all the time.

He does it when we get to the bay at Palma, just as the sun is starting to slip down the back of the world.

He says, 'You got a favourite part of the day?'

I say, 'Yeah. 2.14am.'

'I'm serious man. Don't you appreciate sundown?'

'Of course I appreciate sundown, but there's some decent fucking noons too. It depends on the day.'

He goes, 'You're such a dick, you dumb Irish turnip. What I'm saying is, Baker, this could be the best time of day on the best day of your life, you freaking idiot. Look at this shit. Breathe this crap in for a minute. Lick it up for a while.'

And, you know, he's right. In fairness, this could be a contender for something of all time. Colour, smell, temperature, place – this stuff could top a couple of lists if you're writing lists.

And it hits me.

He's made me feel a moment.

He's made me stop.

Standing here, now, somehow makes me feel like I've come to something.

I've never felt that before.

The money I'm getting.

The beauty I've seen.

The end of the shite I've had to deal with.

It all becomes clear in a spectacular moment.

Me and the world find ourselves face to face, both smiling.

Nap walks us to the yacht, all the way past a line of yachts, a success of yachts, past millions and millions of dollars of yacht, yachts all spot-lit by the wide red sun. They all glow a fierce, dreamy orange, some kind of warm welcome from the people at the top of the money-tree.

I feel the hairs go up on every part of me when I see *The Sand Bed*, the Sheikh's boat, the longest, highest, cleanest, whitest, widest vessel in the place. It's heavy with luxury, loaded with comfort. Behind those black portholes, behind the long, gleaming cabin windows is some kind of final word on status.

I feel like I need to sit down before getting on board, like I need to take all of this in before committing to moving ahead, to making it real.

I'm pretty sure that's Ratface's hand on my arse as we stand here, stuck inside our suddenly pitiful clothing, looking at this motherload of riches.

A man in white comes onto the gangplank and salutes us, the dropping sun making him unearthly, like a red and orange man from the horizon.

He steps away as the Sheikh appears behind, even more in white, his hands out, a burning halo around him, smiling his welcome like Jesus the man.

He has a captain's cap on, over his headdress, the god on this magic bus to fuck knows where.

I feel the little hand on my arse again, but I let it go.

'I'm letting that go,' I say.

'Yeah,' he says. 'I'm just having a moment.'

'Jesus, I know,' I say. 'This is my favourite part of any day I ever had, apart from you touching my arse.'

In a few minutes we are learning this spotless 80-metre machine has 20 staff and eight guest bedrooms, all doubles. We are nodding as we're told it has a large Jacuzzi on top and – I swear – a helicopter landing pad up front.

We are thinking it's good enough to raise a family in, to ring the globe in, to die in. We all want to own it, to be nowhere and everywhere in it, to make love in every room in it, to tell everyone we're on it.

I don't know how many millions are below my feet but these feet are walking very fucking softly because my heart is slamming with the irrational terror that I might break this thing.

We set sail twenty minutes later as the sun warps into the horizon ahead. A girl with a brilliant bottom in brilliant white shorts serves us a vivid sundowner cocktail and I will not say no.

Sheikh Alam says it's like we're chasing the sun, running for the end of the world, something many men had tried and failed to do before.

'We can't catch it, gentlemen,' he says, the big ball filling his mirror sunglasses. 'We are too slow. Maybe we are too relaxed.'

'Who needs the catch, man?' says Ratface, round shades, wind pushing the last few strands of his hair around. 'I just love the chase.'

We're on the bottom deck, back bar, luxury recliners, cloudless above, polished glass table between.

Sitting opposite me with a grin as big as a bendy canoe is Howard 'Nine Hearts' Hazard. We'd said 'Hello again,' had some eye contact, nodded as if to say to each other, 'Isn't this great?'

But we're both wondering something we don't know the name of. Fact is, to be honest, I feel a wee bit glad we aren't going too far out into the deep blue sea, that we have all agreed plans for tomorrow.

So, yes. This is weird. Nap, the Sheikh, Ratface, me and the Bullfight winner Nine Hearts.

Yeah.

I'm going to try to relax completely now.

My favourite actor? That kidney-shaped guy from *Coronation Street*. No wait, Al Pacino. Or that fat one who does whatever in *Two and Half Men*'s house.

No, the doll with the nose like a scrotum.

Aye.

Benny Hill.

Or that guy from Australia.

Colour? Black. No wait, Blue.

Aye.

Memory?

None so far.

Maybe a bit of today.

Us guests go all quiet, we're all a bit surprised, all feeling a tiny bit suspicious, but it's only natural. We're from the real world.

We're just locked up, all wound just a little too tight.

Sheikh Alam is smiling.

It's lovely, but I don't know now if it's fake.

Kind and big and generous and happy – or forced and cheap and wrong and unreal.

Chapter Twelve

It's 3.17am when I break off from the last of the party and hit my berth. The night's been awkward, full of confused laughs and a sizeable charge of drink.

The Sheikh didn't really want to get into the training, just into the doing. He wanted to kick back, chill out, talk shite, spend the evening, consume it like the man who owns it can.

Nine Hearts kept telling him about savouring the first beer, about how to run through three or four more, then about savouring another down the line.

It's a tactic that sounds like crap to me.

The Sheikh repeated he didn't give a shit, that he didn't want to get started yet, that this was a pleasure cruise, that we would get to work at the Gaudí house.

But Nine Hearts kept going, don't savour this one, do savour that one.

Load of balls.

You think you should tell a hurdler to savour his jumps? No. Tell him to clear them. You want to tell a hooker to savour her tricks? No. Tell her to do them and move on.

The Sheikh stopped listening to him, ended up walking around the deck and pointing at shore lights, saying what was what. Ratface followed behind talking about the price of yachts.

I see a text on my phone as I'm climbing into the sack, pissed as a champion, turning the light off.

It says, 'God help you.'

Again, no number.

I'm like, 'Aye, dead on.'

For all I know it could be the sponsors.

Or it could be someone in Derry I've annoyed over the Bull-fight bullshite. Maybe what happened looked so stupid the whole city feels stupid. Maybe they're embarrassed, ashamed tonight of one of their own sons.

I hate starting to think about all of this, that I've let people down.

Or maybe it's not from Derry. Maybe it's a message from the holy crew, the prayer bears who hate sinkers and need all that Hell in their lives.

Here, do me a favour, will you?

Right?

If I ever turn religious, if I ever get Saved, do this favour for me, right?

Baptise me in deep waters. Take me way, way out and baptise me as deep as you can.

I need to piss right away after lying down. I look around in the half-light and can't see the bog. Isn't there a bog in this room? It's supposed to be a big room, does that mean it has a bog?

It's bound to have a bog.

I know fuck all about yachts.

How many rooms on a big bastard of a yacht are en suite?

Balls.

I can hear a couple of people moving around in the corridor, so I'll wait for it all to go quiet.

I hope in the meantime that I'll fall asleep, that my bladder will doze off for the night and that I kip lovely and madly without pissing all over the show.

I'm drifting away, getting away with bluffing the bladder to sleep, when I hear someone coming into my room. It's hard to tell for sure at first because I reckon the noise could have come from somewhere else. Under the deck those sounds can get all mixed up, the clicks and steps and bangs don't always have proximity or direction.

Also, I'm drunk as a bomb blast so all my senses are blown to bits. But I roll a bit and open my eyes and see a shadow coming close.

In a whisper, 'Baker? You awake?'

Ratface.

Shite in a blue bucket.

'Jesus – what?'

'Just a quick question, buddy.'

I sit up. Ratface sits down on the bed, on the edge, at the middle. It's more appropriate for a fella to sit on the far end of the bed, at the feet, if he's going to sit on another fella's bed at all. In fact it's not really appropriate to sit on a fella's bed at all, unless he's in hospital.

'Go away, I need to sleep here. It's not a hospital.'

I'm pissed off, groggy, tired, full of booze I shouldn't have had. My skin is sticky, moisturised with gin. I need a slash. I haven't exercised, I've spent a long night talking bullshit with people I know I really need to get away from, which is the fucked-up reason I'm here in the first place.

This crap, this Ratface crap, I don't need.

He goes, 'Just one question, man.'

He's drunk as hell. He hardly ever gets drunk, but he's drunk as a scribble. He's a bad drunk, a persistent-talker drunk, a *pssst* in your ear drunk, an explain-everything-ten-times drunk.

'Get the fuck out, right,' I say. 'Get the fuck out or I'll smack you in the gob.'

'*Shhhh*. No don't. Don't do that. Just one quick question.'

I see his hands up now, defensive. 'Don't strike me Baker. That's not cool, man.'

'It is not cool to be sitting on my bed when I am trying to get some sleep. I am exhausted, right.'

'*Shhhh*. One question.'

'Ask the fucking question.'

'Okay. Do you think I look like a rat?'

'Is that it? That's your question?'

'Yeah. That's my question. Do you think I look like a rat?'

'Christ.'

Ratface is known to be sensitive about this stuff, deep down. He is pretty front and-centre with most things, but he has a couple of complexes built in at the back. He's been known to whine on about his inadequacies and worries to the point where people have wished he was dead.

The rat thing, I'd heard, bothered him most.

'Well, do you?' he says. 'Do you think I have a profile like a rat?'

'No. You don't have a profile like a rat. Can I sleep now?'

'Bullshit. I have the exact profile of a rat.'

'You're a man. A man and a rat are two different animals. They're a different shape. You don't see a rat with a beer belly. What you are is a man with a profile that includes a beer belly, right?'

'Bullshit. A rat is called a rat and I am called a rat because I have a face like a rat.'

'No one calls you rat.'

'Yeah they do. In fact it's worse than that. They call me Ratface. I know it.'

'Not to me, they don't.'

'Baker?'

'What?'

'Do you call me Ratface?'

'No.'

'Is that the truth?'

'No. You would have heard me, sure. Have you ever heard me say out loud "Hey, there's Ratface"? I've never done it.'

'I believe you, brother.'

I feel his hand searching for my hand, searching for the shake. Then I feel it isn't searching for my hand, but trying to scurry under the covers.

I say, 'Get off my bed and get out.'

'I just want to shake your hand! Man, you got issues!'

'Get out, you fecking ra— Get out.'

I can see his head shaking as he stands up.

'Baker, you're a freak,' he says. 'A real freak. And I know now, as a matter of fact, you nearly called me Ratface there – to my face.'

I say, 'Yeah, right to your ra— Get out.'

Ten minutes later, I'm trying to doze, and the door slips open again. I feel him coming in, feel him taking a moment to let his eyes adjust.

Christ.

I'm wrapped up tight in my bed, desperate for nothingness, and I cannot have this.

I pull the covers in closer.

And he's still standing there.

The bastard.

For fuck's sake.

And I find the energy I didn't want to expel.

I sit up, furious, and say it loud, 'Get the fuck out of my room you rat-faced freak.'

And as the door closes, I can smell her . . .

Chapter Thirteen

We take a long limo back to the big Gaudí house and wonder what the hell that yacht shit was all about.

The ten-tonne iron gates sweep open and those two mean men in dark suits and shades do their looking as we pass through trees and zig-zag up to the house.

It was getting murky the last time and I didn't get a good look at the grounds. All I could remember was that demented building, the bendy walls, the curvy window frames, the sloping roof, the way it looked like a giant, flashing, fountain-spurting toy melting in the sun.

Now I see how the massive gardens are landscaped by someone whose mind has exploded.

There's little beehive-shaped huts, faces on them like hunched-over people, dropped all over the grass. There's little distant plains of desert with taps sticking up out of the sand, with splashes of greenery shouldering into them. Clusters of trees are scattered here and there, as far as the eye can see. To one side of the house, half a mile away, there's what looks like a full-on wild west forest, all these thick trees wearing giant Stetsons, their arms in the air, maybe about to soak up some lead.

Right in front of the house there's a centrepiece black Buick, bushes and water tumbling out of the windows like it's just been pulled from an untended river. A police light is swirling on top, making the whole bonkers thing some kind of mad art emergency.

On the back end – I promise – a fake dog has its mouth around the exhaust pipe and – I swear – is breathing in and out, eyes corkscrewing in different directions.

'Jesus Christ,' I say, rubbing my head. 'Sheikh Alam you are one deep bas—' and Ratface elbows me in the ribs.

'Yeah,' says Nine Hearts, sitting on my other side. 'Someone's sprinkled the loopy dust over this whole place.'

'Aye,' I say, laughing, one eye on the silent, contemplative Sheikh up front.

Ratface elbows me in the ribs again.

I know now I will not get this week over without punching him in his bastard toothy visage and calling him Ratface.

Brunch is already served on the top of the house. Luckily the sloping roof has a big, level platform, a low wall around it, violent-looking plants in pots everywhere.

'That's not a good wall for someone who is planning some heavy drinking at this elevation,' I say to the Sheikh.

I'm serious.

He pats me on the shoulder.

'If I fall off someone will catch me,' he says.

'Right,' I say. 'If I fall off I'll just die.'

Ratface shakes his head, heaping tapenade onto his plate.

'Your social skills are getting worse by the minute, Baker,' he says. 'You need to drink more.'

The Sheikh laughs, moves away, loading up his plate.

I reckon I might kick Ratface off the fucking roof as I shout the name.

But it's true. I'm knackered. As a direct result the effort behind my will to bond with everybody is dwindling, basically sending whatever social skills I have down the pan. They'd never been much up the pan in the first place, to be honest.

Ratface says, 'I got another freaky text, man. You get one?'

I reckon I did. I reckon I got another one too but, like with the one before that, I don't want any stressing about it.

I say, 'I heard there's some crank sending shit to sinkers. No biggie.'

'Bullshit,' he says. 'You're a fucking bad liar, Baker. You got it too. It said "God help you." You got it, didn't you?'

I chew on some sweet, fresh bread and nod.

'Aye,' I say. 'Well, you know what they say about sticks and stones.'

'Yeah,' he says, 'they break bones. You're full on shit at taking the sting out of difficult situations.'

He piles tapenade into his mouth, looks around at who's here. He clocks Sheikh Alam, Nine Hearts, a woman pouring big glasses of water, then back to me.

'Mark my words, there's a fucking snake in the grass,' he says, bits on his teeth.

Nap arrives up top. I haven't seen him since he took an early night on the boat, drunk as a hatchet. He looks bad, seriously bad. He looks like he's been rubbed with roasted pig fat.

We get chatting.

'I never drank of the alcohol until Sheikh Alam insisted,' he says. 'I am a good Muslim, but Sheikh Alam started me to drink and said I must drink when he drinking. I was his partner of drinking at months and that was every way intensity.

'I thank Allah he chose to want to drink with pro drinkers because my life was going, you know, out the tubes.'

'Jesus,' I say. 'You still have to drink with him?'

'Yes. When he says so, yes.'

Nap says there's three staff in the kitchen constantly making sure the Sheikh and Crystal have everything they need. They'll be looking after all of us, 24/7, as we sit here and – apparently – earn a stack of cash.

He says there's never less than two security guys at the gatehouse in case someone wants to do a number on the Sheikh. And there are two domestics in the house, working all the time, picking up shit and making beds and serving food. And there's a guy working in the gardens all the time. And four Bullfight girls have been hired as servers.

'The pretty ladies are getting ready now,' Nap says. 'Sheikh Alam has gone to change and wants to begin training after we eat.'

'Okay,' I say. 'That's grand.'

The Sheikh appears again and Nap bows and leaves. I don't know if that's the way it happens or not, if Nap has to keep scarpering around the place when he's at the house, but it looks like it.

Ratface appears, still stuck to the Sheikh like a genital infection. We stand there, looking out over a big green and brown and sandy cartoon sea that's really a garden.

There's a pool behind the property, its floor painted like you're looking down on naked people sitting on a beach.

There's a big red cross in the grass, like a grave, that says 'AG' a couple of hundred yards further into the background.

I strain my eyes and see an elephant rising above some trees, an elephant with skinny lanky long ludicrous legs. I won't be shocked if it's real.

If you were a kid here, every day would be a summer holiday.

'Do you know much about Dalí, Mr Forley,' the Sheikh says.

'Not much. Looper, I think. Spanish. He had a moustache like that Belgian detective and stares into cameras like his brain's on fire.'

The Sheikh laughs.

I can see Ratface shaking his head. 'Baker, you're insane man. This,' he points to the grounds, 'is Dalí.'

'That's correct,' says the Sheikh. 'Your coach is quite right. He knows his art. Mr Dalí designed this land and landmarks personally.'

I'm confused. The names have jumbled in my head.

'So, who made the house again?'

'The house is Gaudí,' says the Sheikh, 'the architect. The land is Dalí, the artist. The property is beyond unique, my friend. It is beyond price. It is,' he whispers, 'a very big secret in this world.'

I nod.

'No one,' says the Sheikh, 'knows for sure.'

'Knows that they made it?'

Ratface says, 'Yeah, Baker. That's it.' He looks to the Sheikh. 'I'd heard the rumours, Sheikh Alam. Gaudí spent time in Mallorca, went AWOL for a while. He was supposed to be here to design some church but ended up designing a house. Or that's how the rumour goes.

'Then, maybe in the fifties, word was Dalí had been asked to design some grounds, but no one knew where they were. That it, Sheikh?'

'Yes,' says the Sheikh. 'You are well informed.'

Ratface smiles. 'I know stuff, man.'

'Wow,' I say. 'How do you keep it secret? I mean, a lot of people probably want to see this place.'

'Dogs,' he says. 'Dogs and guns and fences and a no-fly zone. Without those my time here would be torture. Privacy is where my heart is. No one gets into this property. No one gets to see it without my say so. Mine or my wife's.'

'Dead on,' I say. 'How buck mad rich do you got to be to have your own no-fly zone? Jesus.'

The Sheikh laughs. He puts his hand on my shoulder again.

'I am truly looking forward to drinking heavily with you my friend,' he says.

'Me too,' I say. 'You're a good host.'

I've been wondering about his wife, wanting to see her face. I've been wondering if she's at the house, if she was really on that yacht or if Ratface had just found some of her perfume.

I reckon the Sheikh might have told her to stay away for a few days and there's nothing I can even say about that.

The domestic who spoke beautifully from beautiful slow lips comes out with another woman and they clear everything away.

'It is so lovely to see you again, Mr Forley,' she says, as serious as Ebola. 'Was everything okay for you?'

I reckon if I say 'no' she might top herself.

I look at her lips for a while, then into her eyes. I feel a big smile pull along my face, like it's going around the sides of my head.

'Perfecto,' I say. 'Just perfecto.'

She beams back, happy as birthdays.

Knackered or not, I think I might just be chilling out and cheering up.

The four servers arrive, Nap speaking fluent Spanish with them as he guides their way. Sheikh Alam has decided their dress code – sky-blue tops and white shorts, all a hundred sizes too small. I can tell he wants to set the scene. They stand in a line to the side, hands behind backs and look the real pro deal.

Ratface begins to move into character like I knew he would. He has us all line our chairs out to face him, the grounds splayed open in the background behind like he's in some kind of surreal painting himself. He looks every inch the part.

'I'm going to say this now with the greatest respect,' he says. 'Two of you are pro drinkers. Two of you are not.'

Nap drops his face to the floor, maybe a little shamed. He's generally looking more nervous now than hungover, or maybe a bit of both.

Ratface goes on, 'One of you is our very generous host.'

He gives a little bow.

The Sheikh gives a little nod.

'But,' says Ratface, 'if I may, I'm going to discount all that. All of us are going to start at the start. And you, Nine Hearts, whatever you name is – no offence – could do with some extra training. You only won because Baker "the Reactor" Forley was put out early due to the heat issue and shit.'

Nap bows his head in shame again.

Everyone is bowing.

Nine Hearts shrugs, twiddles with an ear.

'But all of you are,' says Ratface, 'from here on, my students. What I propose is to do some coaching then, later, open the floor. Maybe let Baker run through some ideas with you, based on the kind of stuff I've been talking about.'

The Sheikh nods that this is cool.

Everyone nods.

I nod.

'Good,' says Ratface. 'Then I'll begin.'

He looks at the garden, a little wind in his little hair, some sun on his teeth. It's a pregnant pause, and it works beautifully.

'Our sport is called Sink,' he says. 'Our players are called sinkers. We are in a professional business, it is a professional business, and anyone who has a problem with that has a problem with understanding the English language.

'Our business is simple. Our business is the art of consumption. It is not the art of utilisation, but consumption. It is a method of disposal, or, if you prefer, an art of destruction.

'The aim of the game is to, in effect, gentlemen, repeatedly delete that which is put in front of you as efficiently as possible and in a timely manner.

'The other facets to the game – the wordage, the bravado, the eye contact, the machismo – are, at this stage, irrelevant. They are the wrapping, the tinsel, the confetti.

'Nothing is more important in this game than removing liquid from a glass at a consistent and, ideally, swift pace.

'And,' he says, pointing at Nap, 'what is the most efficient way to do that?'

Nap looks around, baffled.

'I drink some now?' he asks.

'No ...' says Ratface, '... doesn't matter. The most efficient way to do that is ...' he walks to one of the servers, a sleek-faced, sunglassed firecracker, and she hands him a filled beer glass from the chill box on the floor, '... is to do this.'

And he turns it upside down.

The beer drops.

It slaps the roasting tiles.

The Sheikh claps.

He is, literally, on the edge of his seat.

Ratface says, 'So, gentlemen, after seeing that and knowing what we know about gravity, we can conclude that there is technically no problem in getting the liquid out of the glass at a fast, consistent rate.

'The one and only problem is that the rules say the liquid we have just seen go onto this rather awesome flooring must go into the mouth. And from there it has to go into the throat and then into the stomach and onwards.

'And that, gentlemen, is where the one and only problem in playing this game arises. The problem is that the human body is temperamental, weak, ill-equipped for fast and sizeable consumption and, much as the brain might seek it, we cannot easily handle it without getting stupid.

'The human, gentlemen, is the problem. I like to think that the player is the only thing in the way of this game being the most simple, perfect, beautiful thing in the world.

'The player is the thing that swallows slowly, that fills with and expels gas, that rejects and ejects, that fails, that thinks too much, that wants to walk away.

'The player, gentlemen, is the freaking thing that gets weak and drunk on this stuff. The player is the problem, so he must be the solution too.

'And that, gentlemen, tells us where we must start. We must, very simply, make our bodies better able to cope with drinking.

'We must remove all the complications and make them perform with more simplicity, with less drama, less output, more input. And luckily, there's an app for that. It's called you.

'What it all comes down to is a mere matter of changing your habits. And if there's one thing the human body can do, it is develop habits. It can adapt.

'Anyone who knows anything about the history of our species knows that very, very well. Anyone who knows anything about the history of our species is minded to say, gentlemen, that nothing is impossible.

'They say you can't drink such and such an amount because it will kill you? Bullshit.

'They say this game is unnatural, that it demands too much from the human body? Bullshit.

'They say this game is for losers? Bullshit.

'Only the very best, bravest and, goddamn it, progressively minded believers can be pro drinkers. Everyone else is just being used by alcohol. Everyone else who drinks large amounts is indisciplined.'

I know Ratface's words well. I've heard them many times. I know his little games, his actions and convincers. I know how he can, piece by piece, dress this game up so it's the finest, most exciting, sweet and beautiful thing in the world.

I've been an admirer of his work in that way for a while, and had been sold the day I was introduced to him, when I'd showed an interest in turning pro at a sinkers' roadshow in Derry.

First thing he ever told me was he didn't want to know me. He said he was fed up with alcoholics coming to him, hoping he would teach them how to get into a fairytale world filled with alcohol. He said they were like thieves trying to get a job in a bank.

I told him I was no alco, that I was in the middle of quitting. I said it had hit me how I was one hell of a drinker, how I had been quitting, calling time on what was actually a talent, how I was ending it when I was still a guy with a passion to succeed at something.

He nodded, looked at me like I was an idiot and gave me £20 and left me, bewildered, standing there, holding a note. He turned round and, walking away, said, 'Buy a bottle of vodka son, see if you keep it close to you and not drink it.'

And I did.

He rang later, 4am, got me right out of bed.

I didn't know if I was angry or not.

'I'm expecting you have a bottle of vodka close to hand,' he said.

I said, 'Yeah. I do. I didn't open it.'

He said, 'Twenty shots, the whole bottle. Now.'

I said, 'No problem.'

He listened as I started putting that thing away. He asked me to count, to add stuff up, to tell him a joke, to tell him about a fight I'd had, to do the alphabet backwards, to tell him why the best song of all time is the best song of all time.

He asked me to make up a story about the moon, to explain how it would feel to be lost in the desert. It was all fine. I was buzzing. I did the twenty shots, couple of minutes.

'Okay,' he said. 'Come see me at the hotel, 9am.'

I said, 'Dead on. Will do.'

My mother had heard it all.

I heard her crying.

I couldn't stand it, went downstairs, fell over in the kitchen and shouted back up, 'It's all good – nothing to worry about.'

I got down the last picture of my dad and told him what I had done, what I was planning to do.

I had to tell him the law wasn't for me, that when I tried to do miracles for people who needed them I always ended up doing more harm than good. I told him my ambition came and went like day and night, that I'd tried and failed to commit to study. I told him I was lost and getting more lost, and that I thought I had found something, one thing, I could hold on to.

I hoped I would hear him tell me all that was okay, him saying that only I knew what I should do. But I could only hear my mum quietly sobbing upstairs.

I excuse myself and go to the bathroom. I can't see one on the top floor but I'm happy to wander a little, get a feel for the shape and depth of this whole place.

I go down a flight of stairs which opens onto a big hall.

One of the security guys walks past along the bottom. He looks up, waves a little. I see his eyes, high fired on something. I see he has a picture in his hand, something printed from the web.

'Excuse me,' I say.

'*Sí, señor*,' he says, stopping, turning, waiting for me to get to the bottom.

'The picture,' I say.

'*Sí*, this?'

'That fella? The guy in that picture . . .'

'Oh, maybe it is that you know him, señor. We keep the picture of everyone who is allowed through the gate.'

'He's allowed in here? Jack Melody is allowed in here?'

'*Sí, señor*. He is expected at the house.'

'Really? When?'

'I don't know that much. Whenever he arrives.'

'Jesus. What's he doing here?'

'I don't know. Is not my business, *señor*.'

'Okay,' I say. 'That's strange.'

'*Sí*.'

And he nods, pupils like pinpricks, walks on.

Jack fuck-face Melody.

Jack asshole Melody from PDTV.

This is really not good.

I sit on the shitter and can hear the voices and chuckles on the roof being carried on the breeze. I enjoy this distance, this space. I could lock myself in this grand bog for an age, get distance and space from this crowded day.

It's as big as a truck stop, this bathroom. There's a phone, cologne, a TV, hi-fi, wi-fi, paintings and a shelf with spring water from Iceland. There's two windows, one that looks out at a lake shaped like a question mark, another looking at four distant wooden robots taking off their hats and putting them back on again. I can't remember if the craziness is Dalí or Gaudí and I reckon it doesn't really matter.

And I sit here, happy enough, pondering art and artists and expelling anything I can.

I'll end up a chalk outline on a toilet floor some day, I reckon. Some guy will be saying, 'He did it his way, he got his bit of space.'

My mobile rings. It's Barry, the manager at Darby O'Kills.

Oh, fuck's sake.

I brace.

I face the music.

I go, 'Well, horse?'

He goes, 'How's it going? That was some fucking disaster then.'

I tell him it wasn't, it was a setback, it had nothing to do with my drinking, it was external circumstances. I tell him how good it had all been going, that ironically it would only help make my name, that I'd already been asked to do some training.

I sound like I'm reading it.

He says he knows all about it, that everything's going to be okay.

I smile.

I say, 'What's the story then? Are people fucked off with me?'

He goes, 'Aye. Fucked off but to be honest they're still a wee bit proud, don't worry about that. Derry's had worse people. You weren't actually beat by the bastards, like. You weren't beat in the drinking, like. So you're still on-the-up to us. You can't just be expected to pull a big victory out of your hole a few months after going pro, like.'

I go, 'Dead on.'

It's great to hear.

He says, 'Can you plug Darby's a wee bit more, like maybe at any press conferences or if you're interviewed and stuff? Top singles bar in Derry and all. Fucking place is half dead at night.'

'Business bad?'

'Aye, same oul skint perverts scratching their balls, same oul drunk dolls lying around like fish suppers.'

'Right,' I say. 'I'll do my best, Barry. You're a good man. Cheers again for the support.'

And now I'm thinking how if I get this 100k from the Sheikh, if it all gets put into Ratface's account and he coughs up my share, I might never need Darby O'Kills' money again.

I'd throw Barry a few quid though.

There's a text waiting when we end the call.

It goes, 'No planning, no point, no future . . .'

I look at it, number unknown.
I wonder has Ratface got the same one.
And then I hear him on the breeze.
He goes, 'God fucking damn this bastard!'

Chapter Fourteen

Nap comes looking for me in the bogs, just to check all is okay.

He comes to the door, says he's waiting in case I need anything.

I reckon it's the howling stench of my shitting that makes him think something might be wrong.

He confirms, saying, 'I'm sorry but it is the private human scent that is much very strong so I just want to know, in case of you need medical support which I arrange no problem.'

I say, 'No thanks, but that's very good of you.'

We pause and I drop one.

Then I say, 'I'll spray some of this stuff in the flowery bottle round the place when I'm done. I don't mean to stink your house up.'

'Please don't worry about anything like that here,' he says. 'Be free, Mr Forley.'

'Okay. Thanks.'

I spray some of it anyway and wash my hands with this amazing soap that feels edible, feels like a marshmallow.

I splash with some expensive and look at myself in the mirror.

I'm a raw version of me.

I wink, and hate myself for it.

I'm out and saying to Nap that a sinker's body needs to express itself a lot. I tell him all is well, that there's no shocks, that you get to anticipate what its reactions will be to what you have been putting into it.

'Just because you take a lot of liquid on board doesn't mean to say a lot of liquid will come out,' I say wisely. 'It can come out in a variety of forms.'

He's nodding, respectful and interested.

He's leading me back upstairs to the roof bar, taking two steps for my one step. It strikes me he's flawlessly and politely high-speed fascinated in everything anyone is saying, all the time.

'You know great deals of material, Mr Forley,' he says. 'This is why Sheikh Alam is most very interested in your skills and the adventure of careering to this day.'

That's great, I think. Good to have a fan like the Sheikh.

I think about the money for a second, but only for a second.

I say, 'Let me ask you, Nap, was this invite coming anyway, even if you hadn't decked me?'

'Yes,' he says. 'Sheikh Alam will say if you ask to him. Do you know he had been speaking to bring you here and offering massive riches of sponsoring for you, Mr Forley, so you have no more Darby O'Killing on your T-shirt.

'Then it was changed when you stared at the face and breasts of his lady wife. He would meet you at first instead, to see if you were a cracked pot or not.'

I think, 'Fuck' and 'Balls'.

This could have been so much simpler.

Oh well.

My fault.

But still, maybe I can still walk away from here with a big sponsorship deal.

I ask Nap about Jack Melody, if his PDTV people are coming to the house. He's stumped.

'I don't know of that,' he says.

'You know, if my manager finds out Jack Melody is coming here he will go bat-shit and ape-shit and horseshit and worse.

'I'm telling you Nap, he will push that dickhead off the roof. There's bad history there. He can't stand him.'

Nap goes, 'I don't know about it, Mr Forley. I will go see and attempt to find, but if Sheikh Alam has making not to tell me then that is the way it must certainly be. I would never be asking to seem to question his business, do you see?'

'Yeah, I understand. Well, see what you can find out.'

Up top and the Sheikh is mad keen to hear me speak and watch me drink.

He loved Ratface's words, the pep-talk about how being a sinker is the same as being a genius or an athlete or an inventor.

Ratface says being a sinker means being some kind of deity. He told me one day, 'My favourite moment of all time was when I realised that a man can grow strong on what makes other men weak. I realised that day that one man can turn the whole world on its head, that a man can become a god.'

I slip my shades on and take the floor where Ratface had stood.

I nod and bow at the Sheikh and talk a bit about my style. I say in the early stages of play one of my tricks is to make each mouthful a little bigger than the last. I tell them I focus on my hand, mouth and stomach and that, mentally speaking, the throat is not part of my play, it's just some place the liquid passes by.

I say, 'I feel the stuff in my mouth then send it running. I feel it in the stomach and then I'm ready to hit again. I forget about the throat. It's not important. Commit, down, clear.

'One other thing I like to do is to seize the glass, to commit, before I'm ready. I like to tell my body it's ready before it's ready.

'That way your body gets into the habit, it starts to do what it knows your brain wants to do. Body obeys brain as sure as night follows day. Drive from the brain and you'll soon see the body has no choice but to follow.

'I like to aim for as much emotional control as possible, to build and build on it. It's what you need in this game. Master yourself so you can master the circumstances, the environment.'

I say it's good to get to know yourself drunk, to get blitzed on beer, then on whiskey, then on vodka. I say take each experience out into the street, into the shops, into the bank.

I say go play poker after seven hours of drinking. Call up some old school friends after fifteen pints of Guinness. Take a mountain bike to a park after thirty brandies. Film yourself telling yourself what's going on at the stage when you know you won't remember even doing it. Write about everything when you're out of it, then write about it again when you're back. Get used to working, concentrating, planning, when your head is a fucking bun.

'Get to know each feeling,' I say, 'to know what to expect from it, to learn your limitations, your strengths and weaknesses.

'Sink a bottle of straight gin on an empty stomach then do the same after packing up with carbs and see the difference. Feel where it burns you, then feel where it fills you quickest.

'You've got to get to know every little millimetre of your insides, of your bladder space. You've got to get to know what makes you shake, what makes you smile, what makes you need a shite, how long you can go until you have to piss.

'Savour every flavour, learn what they are, what they make you think of, what they mean, what they are likely to make you need or want to do.

'You've got to get to know what makes you angry, sad, stupid, slow, happy or smart. You have to soak yourself in this stuff, so you do. You can work with it by understanding it. You can't beat it, you can just learn how to roll with it, how to manage it, how to let it be part of you and have no questions to ask it and none left to get asked by it.

'Think of it as being nothing to do with learning about alcohol, but learning about yourself, who you are when it comes to getting different kinds and different amounts of stimulus.'

Nine Hearts says some stuff after I'm finished and it winds me up a wee bit. He says he had more experience than me, more respect for the booze, saying he took more pleasure from it, that he was more of a sportsman.

It's a good strategy for some, I suppose, and who am I to argue with the winner of the Bullfight. But I reckon he's kidding himself.

The Sheikh calls Nap to his side and checks if he had ever tasted straight gin and Nap says no.

'Try it now,' he says. 'Then describe in fulsomeness the flavour to me. I want to have your personal opinion.'

'Yes of course,' Nap says, and goes to talk to one of the servers about getting some raw gin.

Ratface stands up and applauds me and Nine Hearts.

'Baker was the best,' he says, clapping hard. 'If I may say Sheikh Alam, I taught this guy to do the pro rocking that he does.'

Everyone applauds Ratface because the Sheikh does.

'I propose,' says the Sheikh, standing up, his big arms out, 'that we begin a competition.'

We all applaud that. We are kind of building the habit of clapping every time he says something.

'I propose,' he says, 'we all do some extra learning by talking ourselves through Base, by offering advice to each other. I propose we do this in a friendly, kind manner and enjoy ourselves like gentlemen.

'Don't worry because there is still plenty of time to play hard and aggressively like wolves, and I know you stinkers – ha! – not stinkers, sinkers – I know you will want to do that.

'But I propose a kind stage one with some nice sharp, light San Miguel beer from the Spanish mainland. How do you feel about that?'

We clap.

Nap, sweating heavily in his suit, shirt and tie, has moved in beside the Sheikh, the glass of gin in his shaking hand. He raises it to all of us and we turn our applause on him.

'Many cheers,' he says, and drinks it all under the eye of the Sheikh.

We are all tired after the late night, after the yacht, after sitting for the morning and midday in the sun. We've still had no real break, no let up, since the Bullfight.

I could sleep for Ireland and can only guess Nine Hearts must have wanted to do the same for Israel. But it wasn't time for sleeping or for our feelings to be aired or for our complaints to be logged and investigated. This is business, and we have to put brave faces on.

Ratface is doing good to get into the drinking at all. It was rare for him to lift a glass, and I'd never seen it happen two days in a row.

We build a heavy cadence as we begin knocking away the beers, the four servers getting their first chance to do something other than smoulder in the sunshine.

The Sheikh gets to show off some skills, to show how he really can put them away. There is an enormous stomach under his robes, a vast, rich, happy, all-consuming gut of good steak and cold beers and fat chairs and fashionable artists and lavish beds and punkawallahs and bathrooms.

Nap has gone to sit in the shade after downing the gin, wandering away and bowing at the same time, taking beers with him and promising to catch up. He tried to tell the Sheikh that the gin tasted like some kind of animal urine but that he couldn't be more precise about species.

He apologised and apologised and apologised for apologising and took a sun seat close to the corner of the roof. He didn't jesus, although I thought he might. But he did fall asleep, dog tired and full of booze and servitude.

'I like this man,' says the Sheikh, pointing over to supine Nap. 'He is a good and honourable man. He tells me everything I want to know, he keeps nothing back. He doesn't lie to me.

'Example – last week I was in London and he explained to me that one of my guards there had heard a staff person there say the rich Arabs like me wear these robes so we can shit where we like.

'My Nap told me that the English people there believe I might shit in the lift as I go up and down in Harrods. That I stand there with my legs open and shit because I wear no underwear.

'My Nap tells me they think I wipe my personal body with my left hand and with nothing between my left hand and my personal body. And this is after I take a shit in the lift.'

The Sheikh finishes off his beer, followed by the rest of us. The servers, without missing a beat, snap open the next, fill glasses and place them down in front of us, cats and their fresh kills.

'I tell you only, my friends, that this is not true,' says the Sheikh.

We're relieved to hear it. I'd heard somewhere too some crap about rich Arabs and lifts and left hands.

Sheikh Alam says, 'I only clean out my shit remnants with my RIGHT hand!'

Awkward silence.

'I'm fucking joking you drinking bastards!'

Lots of laughter.

Lots of applause.

Lots of beer.

Lots of heat.

We finish Base, a vodka Ludwig and Gisbourne as it's hitting 4pm. The sun has blunted a little, but it's still big and burning and pointed right at us.

One of the staff had been up earlier, offering sun cream to everyone and I'd had it plastered all over my neck, arms and face. I'd been feeling that way-too-polite warning sign from the skin, that tiny tickly tingle that signals you've got a visitor, you've got some pain coming to stay.

Everyone takes time out to stretch their legs, to let our gluey eyes check each other's state, to see how smashed the other guy is.

I'm okay, leading the pack, but Nine Hearts looks a little lost, a little unrecovered, too much retox before detox.

Nap comes awake and starts apologising and vowing to drink as much as possible.

Ratface has taken a back seat, having quit the game due to an unspecified medical complaint, and has egged all of us on during the three heavy stages.

I lean my head back and look up and burp and think how I'm sunburned to shit. I feel like the heat has been building on me, stacking up on me, that it's heavy on me now, that I don't feel it getting any cooler.

My face burns as I search out the big ball, all hazy and unclear in that cloudless sky, those silly 93,000,000 miles away. I think how I'm seeing amazing stuff with my own eyes, how I'm seeing something that's warmed the faces of cavemen and dinosaurs and everyone who ever lived.

Now I'm thinking it's like a crack shot, that it could blind me from all that distance away. I'm thinking it could start sliding over, towards our angry wee rock. I'm thinking how we would all stare up, open mouthed, powerless and awestruck at a moving sun. We could watch the sunglasses melting onto our pissed-up faces from the inside.

The shades never come off Sheikh Alam.

He never stops drinking, clinking, laughing.

I think how he's genuinely high on life, how he uses wealth better than I've ever seen.

I shake myself and head on down to my bathroom, letting the others use the toilet at the top of the house. My pisser is down two flights of stairs and past some statues in that big hall. They stare at me, making me feel human and stupid.

But nothing eyeballs me in my own private toilet. I can do a good, long, easy piss and/or dump in my own private space.

No observers.

No fans.

The simple thought excites me.

On the red tiled floor where I'd seen that security guy walk, I see Crystal. She looks at me as I'm coming fast down the steps, fast like a fella who thinks he knows everything there is to know about the place he's in.

I see a divine naked statue and then I see her.

She's so much more.

'Hey baby . . .'

It's out before I think. It's out and hanging there like a flasher's balls. It's out and cold.

She looks away.

I walk on down. Her hair is exposed. Red, ginger, strawberry blonde. Luscious, shoulder length, healthy, full. Blue jeans, loose but shapely on her high, hard arse. A pink tee, just short enough to get the eye searching for a button.

I'm impressed, or horny, or something.

'Okay, not baby then, sorry love . . . sorry Crystal. You not speaking?'

She turns, walking backwards, shakes her hair.

'Rats don't talk.'

'Come again?'

'Rats don't talk.'

'Right. Depends on the rat.'

'What?'

'Well, some guys are rats because they talk. Italians call guys rats. Rats rat on their friends.'

I'm talking balls again.

She stops. The bold red floor really works for her. I've never seen a woman so complimented by her environment before. If the whole world stopped right now, if the sun rolled over and said 'lights out', I'd stand here looking at this creature for as long as I could.

'Fuck me, Baker,' she says, 'you're a right slow git sometimes. You called me a rat, you prick.'

She throws her eyes up the stairs to check no one's there.

'I did what?'

'You heard me. On the yacht.'

'Wait, wait, wait,' I say. 'I think maybe we're getting mixed up here.'

I approach and explain about Ratface coming in, about how I must have got her and him confused. I say how it was nothing to do with seeing her face. I tell her he's always touching my arse.

I say, 'So what did you come to my room for?'

I'm hoping she says something dirty. Drink does that to a guy. He wants to do some chase cutting. She could say something obscene and I could take her to my bathroom across the hall and bend her over at the window ledge. The four robots could take their hats off to us as we drill and dribble.

'No reason,' she says, but smiles when she says it. 'You're drunk, sportsman. Go play your game.'

'I'm way ahead of them,' I say. 'I can take some time out.'

She smiles and goes, 'Better not. But hey, I like your freckles.'

Fuck sake.

The freckles.

They're out.

It's the ginger thing.

I point a finger in the air.

'No chance of you joining us up top?'

'Nope. Not a woman's place really, unless you're working there.'

'Oh, right. So maybe see you later?'

'Maybe.'

There's one other thing. I have to ask her, it's on my mind.

'By the way, you know anything about Jack Melody coming here? You know, the guy from PDTV?'

'Why? What have you heard?'

'Nothing. So he is coming?'

She doesn't like the question. 'I don't know. I'm the last to know. All I know is that my husband was thinking about buying up PDTV. He knows all the people involved. We go to all the competitions. Maybe that's something to do with it.'

'Right. Maybe it is.'

'Baker.'

'Yeah.'

'If you happen to know some of my husband's business and it's something he hasn't personally told you, I wouldn't mention it to him.'

'Oh, right. Private kind of guy, I guess.'

'Yeah. Private and a bit more temperamental than you might think.'

'Gotcha.'

I watch the Saudi Arabian news in my screw-you bathroom and give my sinker gift to the world.

I see freckles on my nose that make me look like I've stolen a face.

I smear some kind of too-late moisturiser over them and over my neck.

Temperamental, she says.

It means a lot if the temperamental person is an oil baron.

Temperamental and she's leaving her husband's bed and coming into my room in the middle of night.

This is crazy.

I have a pot of dosh waiting for me at the end of this week and I'm doing something that could blow it all.

But, Jesus, she's taking risks too.

She must be doolally about wee me.

So how is it that he wants to sponsor me AND wants to buy up the channel? Is that workable? Seems a bit weird, to be honest.

I notice one of the paintings up high in the bathroom is of toothless oul black and white men wearing caps and drinking bottles of Guinness and I feel all proud.

Chapter Fifteen

The fountain on top of the house explodes at 8pm, rushing up through a giant pipe like a bobsleigh and bursting out, Champagne-style, into the hot evening.

'Holy shit.'

Two people said that.

'Mother of Mary.'

That's Ratface.

Water rips into the sky from a big round pod at one edge of the roof. It's a sight to behold, like an act of nature.

I point out, as a matter of fact, how I'd been sitting on that fucking pod thing about two minutes ago. I say how no one who knew what it was thought to say a word.

Ratface isn't troubled.

He says, 'Baker, that sucker would have turned you into a missile.'

'Yeah,' I say back. 'That would be one major arse wash.'

The Sheikh laughs. He has a laugh like Santa Claus. He says he forgot to tell us the fountain was on a timer.

'I must not forget again to warn of that,' he says. 'I so rarely have guests.'

We're uniformly amazed at this feat of engineering, saying

short sentences and watching as it keeps on pumping those thousands of gallons into the air.

I'm wondering when and where it's all going to come back down.

'It scatters over the trees,' the Sheikh says. 'It slowly moves in a circle and fires ten thousand cold gallons in little tiny seconds. It comes back in sprinkle form, falling on my grass and trees like rainfall.'

He lifts a hand and mimics gentle rainfall with his big, clean fingers.

He says, 'Do not worry, my friends, only the trees and grass get wet.'

Sure enough, trees shake and rustle in the distance, bathed by that thing's almighty load.

'It's like a flippin' weather machine,' I say. 'You control the airspace and the weather in it too.'

The Arab laughs. 'You are drunk, Mr Forley. I can tell you are drunk.'

He thinks that's funny. Everyone does. Everyone's laughing. We are all drunk.

We're rotten, liquored, langered, trashed, wasted, blootered, sozzled, pissed, pickled, hammered and blocked.

Aye.

We're blasted, trollied, sizzled, mangled, pollatic, mullered, wrecked, plastered, buckled, pie-eyed, stocious, inebriated, full of the loudmouth soup and three sheets to the wind.

We'd had Campaign, Fishermen and Father Geoff, stages four, five, six, and the Sheikh has called it quits. He didn't like how aggressive and angry and competitive it was getting, didn't want to go further when the blood was up, said he wanted to save that for another day. He hoped we didn't mind if we just sipped whiskey and chilled out instead. He'd never make a sinker, just an excellent adoring fan.

So we all shook hands, vowed no more personal attacks, vowed no more staring, and we drank whiskey.

Loads of it.

We're bleezin, bluttered, goosed, screwed, boogaloo, minging, minced, clobbered, snattered, slung, lashed, locked, warped, wellied, mottled, monged and zombied.

Aye.

We're banjaxed, hammered, stinking, bollocksed, slaughtered, tanked and cabbaged.

We are drunk, blind drunk and dead drunk. We're legless, witless and headless. We're drunk as a bin, as a bus, as a packet of cats, a bag of farts, a bucket of cocks.

We are as fucked as a fucking biscuit.

Whatever.

We are drunk.

I look at the glass in my hands and laugh to myself.

Fuck only knows what my future holds, but it's making me chuckle to think I might actually be the one holding it.

Ratface is okay. He'd returned to the zone and had a lot. He's had more than I've ever seen him take, but still not enough to fully master him. He's an old pro but also a man on a promise to his doctor never to drink again, a man with a controversial and partly illegal insurance policy meaning he would get a liver quicker than a dying child if he needs it.

And – I'm guessing here – but with likely stage-something sclerosis, he may well need it sometime soon.

He's returned now to the water, to chewing pills the size of flash drives and taking the piss out of everyone.

Nap had woken and jesused over the side of the house, scaring the shite out of one of the security guards patrolling down by the front door. He had looked up and squinted into the sun and, I'd guess, must have seen a fat little gargoyle spewing down.

But I have to hand it to Nap because he came back for more, like a pro. He didn't want to let the Sheikh down and he stood back up, wiped his mouth and put the other hand out for a glass.

Nine Hearts had got into a fight with Ratface over some ego shite. He'd taken exception to Ratface calling me the best sinker in the place, even though Ratface was hardly going to say anything else.

The Sheikh had laughed all the way through, occasionally interjecting to calm things but lapping up the entertainment, giggling gigawatts, all the same.

He guffawed as Nap's eyes twisted in as he tackled a beer.

He laughed like a crazy man as Ratface threatened to batter Nine Hearts around the head with a cold case of San Miguel.

'They'll call it a whole new freaking cold case murder,' Ratface said, front teeth to chest with the Israeli.

The Sheikh told me he thought Ratface was a great guy, a superb teacher, a man who saw real craft and majesty in this sloshy, bad sport.

'Aye, that's true,' I said. 'He's the last of a dying breed, thank Christ.'

Sheikh Alam laughs like a donkey. Everything is a hoot to him.

I felt bad about that, about saying Ratface was the last of a dying breed. I'd say he heard me too.

I watch as Ratface spends a few minutes trying to talk one of the servers into kissing him.

He finds out that's no-go and offers her cash, I think, as a shit joke.

She kicks that away and he starts singing to her in Spanish.

He thinks no one is looking.

I think he's drunker than I thought, or at least more drunk than I've ever seen him.

Ever think how sometimes when you've had a few drinks it's like everything's loud and you're quiet?

It's like two phones got taped to the side of your head, a party going on down each line.

And that's what makes you loud, that's why drunks shout. They think the world is rushing around their head when the world is really just getting further and further away.

Only Spanish Ratface knew to sing was 'Que Sera, Sera', Doris Day. What will be, will be. A sweet song.

Nine Hearts says something to the server as Ratface is singing to her and it all ends badly. Ratface punches him in the ribs. Nine Hearts is about to punch him back decisively but, out of nowhere, drunk or not, that little cannonball Nap appears and bundles both their legs together. The guys fall to the ground, tumbled faster than they could think.

The Sheikh speaks out, calling on the guys not to fight, not to be violent, not to ruin what he said was a 'perfect day'.

I say, 'And this isn't even competition, eh Sheikh?'

He honks with laughter and goes, 'This isn't even competition!'

Ratface and Nine Hearts get back up, agreeing all the way to be friends. I can see Ratface is feeling his age, that hitting something hurt him, that standing hurts him.

Nap returns to the side of his master and is handed another drink.

What will be, will be.

I call to tough little Nap, just to see if he had found anything out about Jack Melody. He half shrugs.

He whispers, 'I mention Jack Melody name in conversation with Sheikh Alam and this is nothing said. I ask him if saw he the Jack Melody on PDTV show, if he saw of him interviewing you Mr Forley.

'He said no. He said he didn't. I say, "You know Jack Melody, Sheikh Alam?" I say "You know push push guy with big face and tablet teeth from PDTV?"

'Sheikh Alam nods his head to me. He says he knows this Jack Melody is but addings he has no care for him.'

I was blocked but I could still see the image of Melody in my mind, of his head on that piece of paper.

I say, 'I saw one of those security guys with a picture of Jack Melody, Nap. He told me he was going to be a guest. No doubt about it. It was Jack fucking Melody, defini-tootly.'

Nap says, 'But Mr Forley, Reactor sir, Sheikh Alam would have said to me. He would not someone coming inside to the house who he does not want to having here. Definitely not, Mr Forley. No, no and no.'

'Well,' I say, 'then either he's bullshitting all of us or Jack Melody is . . . fuck . . . I don't know, coming under false pretences?'

'I assure you, Mr Forley, the Sheikh would not playing with such this. I can almost put my fingers on my soul and say Sheikh Alam did not inviting Mr Melody to this house, but I would not die for it, you see.'

'Well then I don't get it.'

Nap nods. 'The only other way is that it is the workings of the Lady Crystal.'

'Eh?'

'She can invite too. It must be her workings that invites Mr Melody but not given to telling. It could be no one else.'

That's weird.

I don't know what to think about it.

Tonight, in bed, was weird too.

Amazing, but weird.

I was out of it, tongue stuck to the pillow, around 2am. I'd decided not to lock the door, just in case of good things. Ratface hit the hay an hour before me. I knew he'd be dead to the world, that he wouldn't be calling for a small hour sniff of a naked Baker.

But I wasn't naked.

I'd got into the room and sat on a chair and fallen onto the floor. I'd handed and kneed my way to the bathroom on a carpet made of captured clouds and jesused like a diarrheic elephant's arse into the toilet.

I'd stood and counted the blotches from the neck up, came to some agreement with myself about the size of my bloot and I'd held the shower head to my face like a hairdryer for a long time.

I gelled up my Irish hair, ridging it at the top for the first time in my life, and poured some Calvin Klein onto my saturated, stinking, rotting skin. From time to time, I took off a piece of clothing.

When bare naked and fucking cool as a cat, I checked the wardrobes for whatever because I was in a very rich man's house. They were stuffed with boxed-up clothes, brand-new socks and shirts and underwear and all sorts of shit.

Was this stuff for me?

Yeah, baby.

The boxes say it: 'Mr Baker Forley'.

Keep 'er lit and Up the Paddies.

The shoes fitted perfectly. The shirts were my size. The boxers were just right. Everything was just perfecto and easy but surreal as a daydream because I had never in my life worn a £500 shirt, or £500 underwear, or £500 socks.

I felt wealthy and horny.

My brain was warm with the dancing thought that Crystal may well pay another illicit visit. My balls felt like they needed to do some work, to delete some liquid of their own.

I walked around the wardrobes, checking out other boxes of stuff and letting my toes get eaten by the carpet.

I felt sexy as bedamned.

I was as drunk as a banana but I felt alive. I could have bet the house was full of sleeping, arseholed souls. The hours immediately ahead were therefore, I was sure, full of some kind of dirty promise.

I wagged a finger at myself in the mirror and heard myself go: 'Everyone is wiped, everyone is gone, everyone is down. You, my friend, are, my friend, as ever, my friend, the last man standing.'

I wagged it again and said, 'You must not do what you want to do, but I know if you get half a chance you will do more than you must not do.'

I thought that was funny.

The boxers are like some slick shiny design that I could tell would make the most of my manhood, that would show off my lump, my bunch, to any passing Brummie supermodel minded to expose her miraculous boobs. They were new and clean and comfy and somehow sartorially met the need, met my horniness.

Then I was at the light switch, then flat out, my tongue stuck to the pillow.

I think I prayed.

And I woke, silently, feeling the bed dip a little.

'Baker,' she says. 'Baker, it's me.'

My sticky eyes rolled back, right out of a dream about a dream and I could smell her damn half perfectness seated right there by my face.

'Baby,' I said, looking into the dark. 'Baby, I was hoping you'd come and see me.'

I was heavy. I tried to elbow myself up a little, but I was a big sack of burned-up and switched-off.

'*Sssshh,*' she said, her soft hand touching my chest, pushing me gently back a little, stopping me from moving.

'*Sssshh,* freckles,' she said, 'stay still.'

'Crystal, baby, I never said you looked like a rat.'

She laughed, a gorgeous chuckle.

'I know, Baker. No one could think I look like a rat.'

'No,' I said. I was shaking my head, at least as much as I could shake it. 'No one could say that.'

Her cool fingers walked down my stomach, down to my belly-button, down to my bundle, my potatoes.

I slipped one hand along the rich sheets, my pinky stopping at her skin. As my night vision advanced, I saw that slim thigh, that silky white negligee.

I raised the hand, placed it on top of that shiny, toned limb, and it was all okay.

A little breeze blew a curtain back and my nuts started to hum.

A little external whoosh signalled the fountain was still ramming its juice into the wild dark yonder, still bursting after putting out the sun.

It was so damn timely it made me want to cry.

'What the fuck are you wearing?' she said, seeking a way into my tight, shiny, flashy, brand new underwear.

'Some new man knickers from the wardrobe. You like?'

She stopped. She lifted the quilt to take a look at whatever it was had slowed things down.

My unreliable sinker dick was – thankfully – hard, but I didn't need this shite. I hoped I hadn't put on a fucking pair of pantaloons or some bollocks.

'Cycling shorts?'

'Say what?'

'You're wearing cycling shorts?'

'I am?'

'Yeah. Nap ordered everyone cycling shorts. My husband told him to. Something your rat-faced friend said about getting drunk and cycling.'

'Oh yeah, right. Jesus. Your husband is one considerate man.'

'Yeah. Okay. Baker, these are too hard to work with. If I push your stomach down any harder you'll probably be sick. It's bloated out like Christmas as it is.'

I didn't even know she was pressing on my stomach.

'Right,' I said.

'Didn't you notice the big saddle padding under the crotch? They're fucking ridiculous.'

'No, I didn't actually. I think I'm all a bit senseless just now, if you want the truth.'

'I believe you,' she said.

'Right, sure,' I said. 'I'll take them off then.'

'Okay.'

I did.

I said, 'In my mind, Crystal, your breasts are like apples.'

She said, 'Yes, Baker. That's nice.'

Then she gave me a hand job and left.

I lie here thinking about heaven, about nerves and emotions and chemicals and chemistry, and reckon I need one more piss.

I fight myself, fight some sheets and fight a big bed and soon get my feet on the floor ready to stand.

I chuckle as I delight in the fact that my cock had worked, that I had been fit to play the crazy game with her, that my length had been so damn thirsty for her it had performed like a stick of dynamite, like a fucking Hellfire missile in her hand.

I hope I didn't ruin her any lasting impression by wearing cycling shorts. The padding really does make it look like you've messed yourself from behind. A bad choice on my part, all in all.

I stand and walk and look out the window of the en suite bog as I arrive. I feel lighter, happier, higher, more sober.

A man is standing in the courtyard, plain as day, right beside the limo with the shite growing out of it.

He's flicking through his phone, his face lit a moony blue as he's looking down.

There's a whoosh from above as the guy draws on a cigarette. I look as best as I can and I'm pretty certain it's Jack Melody.

I look and look.

Fucking Jesus, I'm sure that's Jack Melody.

I might shout something.

'Hey Melody, you ball bag.'

'Hey Melody – are your teeth size A4 or what?'

'Hey Melody – is that part of a Tesco bag-for-life built into your cheeks?'

But I have to piss. It's been tapping, now it's leaving.

I step back after and no Jack Melody, no man at the limo.

'This is buck mad,' I say.

'Now has that been an intense five minutes or what,' I say.

Going back to bed, an anonymous text message.

It says, 'You are going to die this day.'

I'm like, 'Holy fuck.'

I'm asleep in seconds.

Chapter Sixteen

Pro drinkers can never go back to being amateurs.

Amateurs' enthusiasm is all naïve, childish, exploratory. They want to get drunk, they like to get drunk. Some of them want to get drunk as hard as possible, to remove themselves from the controls.

Pros want to drink as little as possible. We want to be as undrunk as possible. We want as much control as we can get.

Amateurs and alcoholics want to be drunk. Pro drinkers want to be sober.

It hits me at 7.31am that the Sheikh must be an alcoholic. He wants to press and push and slam that booze into him all bastard day.

And he's certainly not an amateur.

No one can *want* to do that, to opt out, to put everything on hold and into harm over and over and over.

Something has to *drive* you to do that stuff.

If it's not competition, it can only be addiction.

So the bedside phone rings.

7.31am.

A million-dollar voice goes, 'Good morning. Sheikh Alam will meet you at the terrace breakfast table at 7.55am before training will recommence.'

'What the Jesus fuck!'

'Thank you, Mr Forley.'

Christ.

This is the bit where I have to remember the money.

I lie here, stewing in a hellish mix of rage, dehydration, depression, exhaustion.

Ratface rings, says, 'Remember the money, soldier. It's discipline or it's disappointment.'

I say, 'This is fucking insanity. Pros need to rest. I'm going mad here, literally losing it. My head is mushed to the balls here.'

He says, 'It's only a few more days, Baker. A few little days to big bucks. Then you can take a month off.'

'A month? Are you joking, you bastard? I'll be gone forever. Bye bye until the end of friggin' time.'

'Yeah, okay, whatever you say. See you at breakfast, champ. And make sure you wear some fresh clothes for once. Check the wardrobes. Loads of cool designer shit for you in there. This guy is the host with the most, man.'

I'm burned out. Burned out, burned up, burned over and burned to shit. I have a shower and shave a face I hate and don't care if I slit my throat.

I slap myself a lot, trying to slam some life into me.

I want to punch myself, to punch someone. I have freckles that make me look like I'm not a serious person, when I'm at this moment as serious as a bomb up the friggin' arse.

'Okay,' I say, telling myself I can calm down, 'not dead, not dying, not done, no complaints.'

I breathe in and out a few big times. I get dizzy and hold onto the sink. I put on a white T-shirt, some long denim shorts, some Moses sandals and head for breakfast.

Everything is being served on the roof under another searing, loaded-air day.

I smell fresh cut grass as I stroll into the picture, the last to appear.

The Sheikh stands up and puts his big arms out to welcome me. He hugs me a little, which isn't the best at 8.01am, but I play the part, flash a smile, sit down.

I'm thinking how his wife had her paw around my shagger just a few hours ago, and I think I'm happy at the thought right now.

We sit in our shades, all pretty quiet, and eat scrambled eggs and toast and croissants and cheese and ham. I eat as much as I can. All of us do, packing in as much as possible into our busted, resentful guts.

We eat tomatoes and salami and melon and fried eggs. We eat bacon and sausages.

The Sheikh won't touch the bacon and sausages, he says, for religious reasons. I look at him and wonder if he shits in lifts.

Nine Hearts has a bacon butty. I think he's Jewish but I don't give a fuck if he is or if he normally eats bacon or not so I stop thinking about it.

I drink no coffee, only water.

I feel now like I might boke.

There would be zero sympathy.

As I sit back and belch, the Sheikh says we're all heading off on a bicycle ride around his property.

For fuck's sake.

No one wants to.

We meet at the front, all changed into our stupid paddedcrotched cycling gear, as a van pulls up. One of the security guard drug freaks gets out and gives each of us a brand-new bike.

The Sheikh leads the way and we pedal gently and wankily for a lap of this wanker land, which will take about a fucking hour.

We pass those four wooden guys taking their hats off and putting them back on again. They're ten feet high and skinny and about as arty as a shit and with less use.

We pass some fake rabbits and a wanky door in the ground that, the Sheikh says, opens onto an optical illusion of the devil looking up at you from beneath a thick piece of glass.

Whatever.

I notice from one angle how a couple of little hillocks in the distance have bushy nipples on them.

'It's like being in a freaking pop video,' Ratface says, pedalling with his skinny, paper-white veiny legs, 'or that *Alice in Wonderland* bullshit.'

I hear him breathing heavy. I am wondering if I'd care if he dropped dead. He's really sweating hard in the mad morning sun, but then we all are. All stuffed and knackered and shoved out of the crap, pretend comfort zones we live in.

This isn't right.

'Yeah,' I say. 'I'm losing the ability to be impressed by houses or land or art or wealthy Arabs or any cunting thing.'

'The bucks, Baker. Your bucks. Come back to earth.'

'I know. Other than that I'd cycle this thing straight off the cliff or under a train or something.'

Then I say, 'So you hear from Jack Melody since the press gig?'

'Melody? Why would I hear anything from Jack asshole Melody? Get a grip, Baker.'

'Dunno. You threatened to slit his throat on live TV. Just

wondered if he'd come back on that, or if you knew where he was or, you know, where he is?'

He goes, 'You're freaking insane. I've threatened to kill that nutsack a hundred times on TV, in hate mail, in email, on freaking Facebook. I've shouted it through his damn front door, Chrissake. I don't give a shit. And I will kill him if I get the chance.

'Anyway, he'll be back in his dumbass Miami condo now. Probably masturbating to flamingos or some shit.'

'Yeah,' I say. 'No reason why he'd still be in Mallorca, is there?'

'Baker. Shut the fuck up. Let's get this bicycle shit over.'

'Okay.'

'Today we'll breeze over some wordage stuff with the Sheikh. Kill some time. Then let's get Nine Hearts to speak some more of his bullshit, pretend we're into it. The damn pansy. Just let the Sheikh watch and we'll try to get some rest.'

'Right. I'm up for that.'

'And lay off with the Jack a-hole Melody shit, Baker. Even the name hurts my damn ulcers.'

I shower again, change again, drink three litres of water and might throw up again.

I wonder how much thinking I need to do about the Jack Melody thing, or if I need to think about it at all.

I consider how I'm no detective, that I'm sharp but I've no mental rigour, no decent mental stamina, nothing making me not want to stop thinking.

I think how I'm not at all nosey, that I don't really give a shite about what's going on in the world and how sometimes I think everyone on the planet can go fuck themselves.

Against that background, it's hard to be too bothered, hard to remember to even keep thinking about Jack Melody, let alone work out if I should land some more fact checking shite on Nap.

And – just to check – I did see him, didn't I?

It is him who's been texting us, isn't it?

Ratface told me one time he and Melody fell out big time over a scam they pulled back in the States. Melody was a respected TV sports reporter at the time. The plan was he would be the only journalist who witnessed the most intense round of drinking in recorded history, he was going to have the scoop on what was a truly monumental session.

The idea was to be that death itself had been beaten back, that there had been some kind of angelic interference as two hardcore pro sinkers, fired up on mad competition, drank beyond the bounds of biological possibility, beyond reason.

Yet these two legends were to have drank themselves into a state of singular clarity, a state that somehow moved beyond the influence of human frailty, beyond what alcohol can offer, which ended only when they both stopped drinking at the same time and, momentarily, both said they had witnessed something above the understanding of man.

Basically they had met god, or some kind of god, while utterly bazooked on the shitty beer and whiskey range that Ratface was about to launch.

Oh yeah, and Ratface had some quack off the telly who was going to say the guys' livers were in great shape, as if the experience had been not just spiritually healthy, but also physically reparative.

I know, fuck sake.

Yet, as the two well-known sinkers refused all offers of follow-up interviews, you just know people would have wanted to hear more of this bullshit.

Melody, who would swear by what he witnessed, was in for a cut, a percentage of related future revenue. His role was to tell the story, to write the book, to carry out the only verifiable interviews with the two blessed hammerees.

Everyone involved would get paid off and the two sinkers who found a sort of god would, without any further ado, disappear forever, avoid the media forever and forever keep their fully formed horseshit to themselves.

'It was all perfect,' Ratface told me. 'A mystery, a sales pitch like no other. Magic liquid, beautifully, totally and independently endorsed. There's never been anything like that in our crazy trade.

'The press would have wanted those sinkers like motherfuckers, and the harder they vanished, the more the mystery.

'Every story the damn media did would have had to feature that bottled battery acid we were peddling. We were all going to win big, man. I was sure of it.'

Except it all went wrong.

Ratface and Melody fell out at the eleventh hour and the entire scam hit the skids. It wasn't until the night in question, as the fake game began, that the two sinkers found out it had all turned to shite.

Melody never showed for the event and Ratface got seven bells kicked out of him by the sinkers who said the beer tasted like rabbit's piss anyway.

He had to drop the plans for his drinking range and take a couple of years out, mostly in physio, after that fucking hoo-ha.

I asked him, on that one and only time he talked about it, what he and Melody had fallen out over, what was it that made

Melody so bent out of shape that he would smash up that nice, fat gamble?

He didn't answer the question.

He just looked into the distance, grinded his jaw and said, 'I hate that man. I hate his hair transplant, his plastic surgery, his botox, his tombstone teeth, his face, his mind, his life, his family, his food, his house, his friends, his dogs, his socks, his soul, his hi-fi, his . . .'

You get the idea.

The servers aren't here. The Sheikh says they're pissing his wife off with all their tits and camel toes and hair and handing out drinks and she sent them home.

He says, 'She says any woman with those tits and camel foot and hair and the handing out beers in Nun . . . Nun place . . . the fucking England town she came from . . . would be proposed to or drooled at by every man. I think she is jealous. She has sent all my staff away today as punishment to me.'

'Aye,' I say to him. 'Gonna miss those servers though. It's a pain in the arse having to get our own beers.'

The Sheikh laughs. I'm not even joking. I'm so used to having it just when I need it. In terms of time, for a sinker, having to get your own beer is a backward step.

We take our hot stools and get some banter going around the table. I tell the Sheikh how a sinker has got to move every line onwards or else slap it back, how good wordage is about fast entertainment.

'You have to get the guy's words and run them further than anyone else can run them,' I say.

'If you say to me "It's a hot day," I say, "Yeah, going to be 32 degrees Celsius at 1pm and an average of twenty-five dogs and one-point-two kids will be boiled to death in cars in Spain today." Horrible stuff, but it's good wordage. Interesting, fresh, better than yours. You understand, Sheikh? It's about taking the line on.

'Else you say to me "It's a hot day," and I say, "So hot that your fat Sheikh arse is going to start sweating and stinking again and then you're going to faint again like that one other time when you drank a shandy you fucking shadow of a sinker – you might as well quit now, you bulbous eejit."'

The Sheikh nods. 'But that's a lie,' he says. 'I have never fainted and I don't know what is a shandy.'

'Maybe so,' I say. 'The fans don't know that. Maybe you have, maybe you haven't. They don't give a flying shite. They just want to know what you're going to say back to me.'

He says, 'I'm going to say you are a liar but it's okay because I know you talk bullshit because you cannot handle your drink you stupid eejit fuck duck man!'

'Bingo to Sheikhy!'

We all clap. It was a comeback of a kind. Needed work, but it was good enough.

I can see there is some style in there.

Oul Sheikh must have laughed for ten minutes.

And, you know, I keep getting flashbacks as I look at his big, nice face. They involve his wife pulling my donkey, and me encouraging his wife to pull my donkey.

I try not to be sad or happy or hate myself or see myself as a scumbag. I hit back at whatever emotion it is that my sloppy brain is trying to foist on me.

Ratface told me one time, 'Some days in this game you won't

know what way is up, Baker. On those days, manage your emotions, make them servants, not masters. Emotions have no damn understanding of the long game, they just want fed right away.'

He told me, 'Kill all sadness and self-criticism, that stuff is the fart announcing the shit, Baker. It'll fuck you up.

'End it. Stop thinking about it, man up, fuck it, soldier on towards the goal.'

Sherlock Holmes somehow comes into the conversation and the craic moves rapidly along to ninety.

Nine Hearts puts himself out there a little saying he and his buddy back in Tel Aviv have been writing a book about Sir Arthur Conan Doyle's great detective.

'You have a buddy?' I say. 'Like a fuck buddy, you mean. A four-legged one, no doubt.'

'Yeah,' he says. 'Your wife.'

I say, 'My wife died last year.'

He says, 'Good. And fuck you.'

Ratface wants to know, 'So what's this bullshit Sherlock Holmes story?'

'Sherlock Holmes and Hercule Poirot and Columbo in the one story. That's the idea. There's a lot of interest.'

Everyone laughs.

Then Nine Hearts laughs.

We all drink and laugh.

Nothing really makes much sense anyway.

Ratface kicks in. He's a nerd with books and movies and shit. He's a nerd with everything. He told me one time he knew the name of every country in the world alphabetically. He told me one time how he was the first person ever to work out that every continent in the world started and ended with the same letter. I told him he couldn't know that he was first, and he told me I was a dumb Irish carrot.

'Hey Nine Hearts,' he says, 'you land-stealing, house-building, motherfucking Israeli ass. What period is this horseshit detective story set in?'

'Dunno toothy,' he says, 'you moronic little gook-beaten bile duct. It's historical. Set in London. Fifties. I can't do the details now, not a good time.'

Ratface starts laughing his arse off.

He goes, 'So Holmes is like a hundred, Poirot's like a ninety-year-old zombie back from death and Columbo is fricking twenty years old. That's one exciting damn premise for a story, man. Better solve that crime quick before Sherlock shits himself, Poirot's head falls off and Columbo has to wave his mama goodbye and go to goddamn Korea.'

Nine Hearts shrugs, 'I can make them any age I like in my story. And anyway, how do you know so much about the age of fictional detectives, you ugly snake?'

'Your wife told me,' Ratface says. 'She reads about them when you're fucking her.'

The Sheikh, like that crazy fountain, explodes. He spits a big, rich, bubbling mouthful of San Miguel right across the table, anointing everyone. He wipes his face and eyes as his laughter finally dips and tapers off.

Everyone looks at him, all of us wiping as well.

'And that,' says Ratface, 'is immediate disqualification.'

Chapter Seventeen

I'm blurred and all smudged up inside when the sting of the sun finally leaves too late in the afternoon.

Blues have turned to blahs, thoughts have no importance and collapse as they form. Pipes ferry the mess of my life in, out and around my insides, over and over, like a cycle, a rhythm, a repeat-until-dead process brightened now only by the occasional passing cluster of words in my head which say something along the lines of 'death may come quickly.'

Here I am, me, once again, doing what I do

We take five and the Sheikh goes to his big, luxury sun seat overlooking the lavish mind-doping gardens.

Nine Hearts and Ratface take to talking clenched-fist shit about detectives.

Nap has a quiet, fast, violent jesus in a bucket he's hidden behind a chair.

I catch his eye. He shakes his head. I nod back.

C'est la vie, mucker.

I grip tight onto the banister on the way down to my bathroom. The house is quieter than ever. I can hear the silence even among the hollow, roaring echoes tumbling around in me as the blood pumps.

In one room I haven't seen before is a plastic breast on a wall. In another, a spiral staircase leading to the letter M on the ceiling. Everything in that room is red, even the books, even the pages of the books. Everything is red except the M, which is green.

I catch my mouth being open and think 'What's the point?' and close it. I leave, face fired with contempt and confusion and drink and sunburn.

I sit down on the bog and my insides come dribbling out. Shit, piss, jesus – it's basically all the one, all heading for any hole that will let it pass.

I've had more than a hundred beers in the last couple of days. I've had vodka, tequila, loads and loads of whiskey. It's hard to count. It's impossible to really know anything.

If I close my eyes and rest I might not open them again.

That would be some kind of bliss.

I steady myself with the walls and the door as I stand up and feel the dizzy. I tell myself some pointing bollocks into the mirror, some stuff about facing all this like a US marine.

I tell myself, 'Not dead, can't quit.'

I say that I am willing to drink myself to death out here on this island. I say I will not jesus before the day's over, that I may have lost my mind but I have not lost my honour.

But deep down I don't care.

And I realise I'm pissing myself as I stand here, freckled and buckled.

Crystal is outside when I emerge, staggering from the toilet, wet legged, a large stain on my character. The room I'm leaving stinks like dug-up guts.

'Baby,' I say, reaching for her, automatically wanting to touch the soft cleanness of her face.

She steps back and I almost fall.

I have to work on my balance. I need to straighten my head and focus. I feel her at my side, my right side, and try to flop an arm around her.

'Jesus, you've got slippy shoulders,' I say, my limb sliding right off.

'Yes, Baker,' she says. 'Let me help you upstairs. We've been looking for you.'

I feel her lightweight, strong arm wrap around me. A tiny tidal wave runs through the liquid in my body as she grips. I suck in my mouth in case jesus arrives, but then I think it won't, and I suddenly know I can hold this and beat this and be better than this.

She helps me get a foot on the steps and we walk, slowly, back up, dysfunctional lovers entwined.

'Have you had anything to drink, baby?'

'No, Baker.'

'Would you like to have a drink with me for old time's sake?'

'No, Baker.'

'Did you tell your husband it was okay for me to come to the house even after I stared at you like a psycho?'

'Yes, Baker.'

'Do you think you might do that trick with the hand and the bedroom again?'

'No, Baker.'

'I can wear the cycling shorts for you, sweetness.'

'Nope.'

'Okay,' I say. 'So are you going to divorce your husband for me?'

'No.'

'If he says it three times then you will be divorced as Muslims, isn't that right?'

'Yes, Baker.'

'Then I'm going to get him to do that. I'm going to entice him into saying that three times and get it on tape.'

'Okay, Baker.'

'It's meant to be, you know.'

'Yes, Baker.'

I don't know why I'm being so lovey-dovey. It's all one-word answers and hand jobs with this woman. It's all pose about the place and marry the rich guy with this doll.

There is no 'Be good to Baker,' 'Be nice to the Irish guy,' no 'Say something interesting to the Derry fella.' There's no 'Throw the Reactor a bone, warm his heart, make a promise.'

It's all chemical anyway, falling in love. It's just a reaction your body has to a chemical combo fired through some part of your system at some time or another. It comes and it goes and it's all as meaningless as beer or cocaine or happiness or sadness. It's all just some combo.

It's all just emotion and you can push it away and replace it.

Emotions follow thought as sure as two follows one.

Now I think maybe I just want to fuck her a lot, and that's all it comes down to. I think this stuff about really falling for her is my body's way of tricking me, of trying to outsmart me, of trying to get me to try to do some breeding because it knows what I'm like.

It knows I'm going to be pissed for years, that my dumb, wrong ambition will kill me.

It knows time is short.

I feel like advancing this theory with Crystal, but I don't know where to start.

And I've pretty much forgotten it now.

We get to the roof, into the oncoming sun, and she closes the door behind. This is the first time I've known her to be on the roof since we got here.

I turn to her, to make an interesting smile for as long as I can hold it. She smiles back.

She's a good fit for the sun.

I turn to walk towards the people and see it's all strange.

Jack Melody is standing with a stubby baseball bat in his hand. Kneeling in front of him with their hands on the back of their heads are my friends Ratface, Nine Hearts and Nap.

They are all looking at me.

I laugh.

I point at Melody.

'Jack arse face Melody,' I say, un-serious. 'Just what this party needed.'

I look at Ratface, swaying around like a weed in the tiny wind, skittered out of his devious mind. He looks very pissed off.

'Jack fucking Melody,' I say, laughing more. 'I knew you were here, you air-brushed bastard.'

'Forley,' he says, quietly, slapping the bat into a palm. 'Get over here and get the fuck down on your knees and shut the fuck up.'

And I start to get it.

'Oh shite,' I say. 'Wait, wait, wait . . .'

'Knees – now!'

'Shite in a bucket.'

I look behind me. Crystal is pointing to the ground.

'Knees, Baker, now. Do what he says.'

'Ah right,' I say, kneeling close to Ratface, knee-walking towards him a little. 'I get it, I get it.'

I don't get it.

Melody has me walk more on my knees, gets me to face the other three. I think I'm pretty stable on my knees, more stable than on my feet. It may be the lower centre of gravity, or some shit.

I look at this trio of langered bastards and I don't think I have ever seen unhappier faces. When a fella's had three hard days of drinking and gets forced into doing some crap he doesn't want to do, it really shows in his eyes.

Ratface says, 'I told you, plain and simple, Jack Melody is an asshole.'

'Yeah,' I say. 'That's true. You have always, always said, "Baker, let me tell you loud and clear that Jack Melody is an asshole of the highest order."'

'Okay guys,' says Melody, 'enough with the bullshit.'

'It isn't bullshit if you are actually an asshole, Mr Melody,' says Nine Hearts, laying a hard, scary stare on him.

Nap shakes his head. 'I also hear about Jack Melody and the asshole.'

Melody smiles, big shiny square panel teeth. If he was solar powered, he'd be filling up the tank as we simmer.

The bat is a half-size, easy to manipulate, or at least easy for a sober man to manipulate. We are like bowling pins around him, all slow, dumb and easy to knock down.

I can feel Crystal behind me somewhere. She's a player in all this, and not on my team, but I can't work out what's going on.

The Sheikh is still sitting in his chair staring out at the gardens, his burnished power all around him.

I can't decide who I hate most, if anyone.

I'm not in the best mood for all this.

We aren't saying it but we all have a feeling we are going die here under the solid sun.

And it's almost totally all fine with me.

Melody nods at me and says, 'Where's your phone, Forley?'

'Up me hole,' I say.

He's down, grabbing it from my back pocket, flinging it towards the other phones, a pile by the door.

I go, 'Arse-groping cunt.'

Ratface says, 'So what's going on, Melody, you asswipe? What's going on, man? We're burning up here.'

'Listen carefully to what I tell say,' Melody says. 'My way or die way, right?'

I say it loud, firing it behind me, 'What's the score here, Crystal baby?'

Ratface is thrown, 'Crystal baby?'

Melody says, 'Shut up guys, I mean it.'

Ratface says, 'Fuck you Melody.'

I say it again, 'Crystal, baby?'

I can't see or hear her.

Nap kicks in, 'What mean, baby?'

'Nap,' I say, 'don't worry, I won't wink at her or anything.'

Nine Hearts goes, 'Hey ass face, my arms are sore.'

'Hey Jacko,' I say to Melody. 'Our arms are sore. What's the craic here? I thought you were back in your Miami condo wanking over flamingos anyway.'

'SHUT THE FUCK UP!'

Nine Hearts laughs. He has a good, rough laugh, a laugh that has to get out, the laugh of a man who doesn't get too scared too long.

Melody swings the bat as hard as a guy can swing it.

He pounds it into the back of Nine Hearts' head, forcing him forward.

A flash of red into the air and I blink.

Nine Hearts bashes nose-first into the hard-painted Moroccan tiles.

Blood leaks, rolling slowly over the detail, running into the grout lines.

We all watch it, nice and quiet.

It changes everything.

Melody steps over Nine Hearts' head and walks between us all, slapping the bat into his hand again.

He has his silence now.

'Ratface, hold up your right fist.'

Nothing happens.

'Do as I say or I'll do that again.'

I nod at Ratface, urging him to do it.

'Me?' he says.

'Yeah, you. Rat. Face.' Melody turns to him. 'Who the fuck do you think I'm talking to?'

'My name isn't Ratface, you rude motherfucker.'

Melody shakes his head.

I say, 'No one calls him that, you prick. It's actually pretty fucking offensive to call a man Ratface.'

'Okay,' says Melody. 'Anyone who's face looks like the face of a rat, hold out your right fist.'

I look over at Nap. Maybe we are both thinking about the Spartacus scene, where everyone claims to be Spartacus to stop the actual guy getting caught. But the mechanics of this situation are different.

Melody bends down, right into Ratface's face. 'I'll put it another way,' he says. 'Francisco Fall, put your fucking right fist out.'

Ratface grimaces and sticks his little right fist out, his little knob shaker, his bottom fiddler, his nose picker.

'Now,' Melody goes, 'I want you to strike this little fat Jordanian lump of shit with it, right on his fat little nose.'

He means Nap. He wants Ratface to hit Nap. It doesn't make any sense.

Ratface speaks, 'He's going to kill us, guys.'

'Shut up,' says Melody.

'He wants it to look like there was a fight here.'

I think for a second and say the only word that comes to mind. I say, 'Why?'

Crystal's legs come into view. One of my eyes slides up her body.

Now I mumble, 'Fucking Nora.'

I can't help it. I want to smile at her, to kiss her ironically among this conflict. I feel like doing a wolf whistle.

Melody again, 'Francisco, hit Nap on the nose or I'll kill him.'

'Do it,' says Crystal.

I sense some kind of difference in her, some new kind of new mood, some kind of nasty.

Nap shuffles around to face Ratface. He looks stern and serious, right into his eyes.

'Do it Francisco no Ratface,' he says. 'Hit me hard as you can. Hit me very hard. Hit me now. Hit me.'

'No,' says Ratface. 'I'm not hurting anyone here except Jack ass-face Melody, the damn flamingo masturbation enthusiast.'

'DO IT.'

That was both Nap and Melody.

There isn't much else to say or do about any of it.

I reckon Nine Hearts is dead.

I go, 'Can we get Nine Hearts an ambulance?'

'SHUT UP.'

Ratface belts Nap.

Tough little Nap hardly reacts, hardly rocks back.

Instead he dives sideways, throws his arms out, reaches for Melody's legs. He grabs him at the shins as Melody swings down for him.

Nap yanks him tight as a bear trap, Melody's tumbled to the floor, flinging the bat out.

Ratface and I try to stand as fast as possible, but Crystal has the bat.

She cracks it on Nap's head, stunning him, loosening his iron grip. Melody rolls away, gets to his feet.

Me and Ratface were just too damn slow.

Ratface goes, 'Baker, you horse's ass.'

He's panting hard.

I say, 'What the fuck did I do?'

'Nothing, you useless freaking spud! You're half my damn age man, you should've been in at him, fixing this shit!'

'Fuck you!'

'SHUT UP.'

I haven't fully got back to my knees. Melody is looking around, panicked at how his crazy show isn't going so well.

I stand on up.

He orders me down, stepping up to me fast.

I stand on up.

He swings out the bat.

I get to my feet and step backwards, then step again, and again. I am running backwards, the bat at my face, wind at my arse.

Sinker

I don't know where I'm going.
Melody stops following.
I hit the low wall, back of the legs, fast reverse.
I get all flung, arms flailing, over the low wall.
Even if I'd had a plan, this wouldn't have been it.

Chapter Eighteen

The word on the street is clear. Pro drinking is on its last legs.

The headlines have been all *Time Please; Last Orders for Killer Sport; Is it finally Cheers to the End of Pro-Drinking?*

There's petition upon petition, terrible tale upon terrible tale and, worse still, the crystallising social stigma that says, basically, if you want to be a pro drinker you've already lost at life.

The halcyon days of the late 1800s, the 1930s, the '40s and the big rebirth of the '70s had all passed and nothing would bring them back.

The sport is beloved by many, but it's no secret that many of the many love it for the wrong reasons.

Pro drinking has become uncool, unclean, unfun, it's hardcore innocence gone.

Pro drinking is smoking, it's slapping your secretary on the arse, it's hairy porn. It's sex without condoms, liquid lunches, cars without seatbelts. It's aeroplane ashtrays, it's farting and failing and unsophistication. It's artless, unprofessional, undomesticated.

It's too stupid and clumsy for cynical Twitter, too ugly and manly and without conscience for Facebook, too slow and dumb for any workable longevity as a sport on the web, to ever get embraced again by the modern chattering masses.

Pro drinking has no CGI, no place in a gym or a coffee house, no hope. It's the easiest thing in the world to look at and say, 'No seriously, they should ban the shite out of that sport.'

And that ban is coming.

We all know it. Few say it, but we all know it. Venues have been getting harder to get, sponsorship is at record lows, membership is bottoming out, campaigns against our sport are constant.

It really doesn't help that the PDA has grown weak, that it went and got all paranoid, that it stopped fighting back as its sinkers, more and more, were just turned into figures of fun, pity and disgrace.

The ban is coming, the tipping point has passed and it will just take something to click everything into place and there will be no turning back.

Pro drinking is in the last chance saloon.

It is off message, bad, wrong, incorrect and it must go.

But you fuckers, you hypocrites, you voyeurs, you envious fucking cowards, you laughing fucking liars – we have our pride, we have our dignity, our outstanding control. We have our history, our culture, our guts, our balls, our fucking wit and our fucking diehard skills.

There are many somewheres at any time of any day when guys like us are the most impressive people in the fucking room. We can clot and blot like nappies – you dull, victim sheep – and we are fearless and strong and real.

You, you fucking enlightened shitheads, just love telling us we're dying when you know, don't you, you fucking ballbags, you corporate tarts, that we are completely fucking alive.

I land on my back.

I get splashed by jesus right on my own face.

I'm winded, struggling for breath with a throat that's coiled and trying to eject.

The jesus punches into my mouth, back down, back up and out.

I roar, I shout the stuff out.

I rub at my eyes, I need to know what the fuck . . .

Everything's blurred, doubled. Two suns are above me, spinning into each other.

I've landed on the roof of a van that delivered bicycles.

I hiccup and I get to take a breath.

I'm alive.

Dung beetle Melody is looking down at me from over the top of the house.

He moves away.

He has to be coming for me.

I roll over and, getting it all wrong, tumble the rest of the way to the ground. I land half on my feet, half on my arse, struggling for a second breath.

I've broken my arm. There's some kind of solid jabbed into my pit now, but I can't look, I won't look.

My drinking arm.

I'm too fucking numb and mangled to get a reliable damage report.

I get up and head, flat-footed, for the front door of the house, for the same place Melody was bound to be headed.

I can only think I've a better chance of hiding inside than out here in the neat madness of these grounds. I want indoors for a phone, a knife, a place to hide.

I want an ambulance for Nine Hearts, a taxi for Forley. I

want to call the cops, to call anyone, to scream something into a receiver.

The door's closed, locked hard.

I look around, fucked.

My arm throbs.

Pain shoots down the right side of my body, and straight back up.

It slaps my head, a headache like a bullet into the brain.

I realise I'm still not breathing.

I start sucking, biting into the hot air, trying to force some of it inside my wet face.

I fall backwards onto my arse and it's like I've been hit by a train.

Yet it has helped, I can feel my lungs move.

I really thought I was dead there for a second.

I stand, slowly, and hobble towards the van.

Locked up, no keys.

I hit dizzy, do a kind of three-point turn to keep me upright, and head towards the grass, towards the trees, into the picture.

But it's all too far, too pointless. My lungs are too weak, my body too broken, my belly too full of beer.

My bladder – now? – is too full of piss. Now? Does it have to be right now?

I'm in the open, running at fuck all speed with water-balloon legs towards something I know I can't reach and even if I do . . .

The only thing for it is the four men, the wooden electronic bullshit pieces of art who lift their hats all bastard day.

The ten-feet-tall men.

The Salvador Dalí men.

Maybe I can get in among them, hang around them, see if they will save me.

I'm running at dead man speed now.

I can hear a door, a shout, commotion behind.

I reach the four men with the hats and I can hear the weird whine of their mechanics as they doff their headgear, on and off, forever and a day.

I duck behind one of them, my breathing immensely loud.

I find this man is ten feet tall tall but ten inches wide.

WTF?

How did I not know that?

No, I did know that.

How did I not remember that?

Anyway . . .

Balls. I can't hide here. I'm a sitting duck. My ginger noggin must be sticking out of the side of this wooden man's legs like pubes from Speedos.

I don't dare look anywhere.

I feel like coughing.

I have a quick look around.

Jack Melody walks, nice and slow, towards me. I don't want to register him, but he's got me.

'Forley, you're a crazy, pisshead, dumb Irish bastard.'

'Yeah,' I say, gasping. 'It's been said before.'

'You really think you can hide behind that thing?'

'It was an idea but I'll admit it wasn't my best.'

'No.'

'Okay, well. Sure, what can you do?'

'You've pissed yourself.'

'Oh, right.' I checked. He was right. And I was still pissing. I keep doing this.

I nod at Melody, suggesting I need to take a moment out. I turn my back on him and, zip down, get rid of it all.

I do it against the leg of one of the four wooden guys and feel ashamed.

I say, 'Sorry there, big fella,' and he lifts his hat to me.

I feel at my upper right arm, feel where it aches, where the break could be. Nothing's sticking through.

'Thank fuck,' I say.

'Yeah, zip it up now Mr Reactor,' says Melody, tapping the bat in a hand. 'Try that again shithead and your brains will be on show like your Jewish friend's.'

He pushes me all the way back up the stairs.

I'm thinking how I weirdly can't tell the difference between drunk and weak. The wanker has picked the perfect time to attack some fellas.

Ratface and Nap are face-down on the ground when I get back up top, Crystal standing over them, avoiding eye contact with everyone.

Flies are sampling the hot pool of blood beside Nine Hearts. They'll be blocked in no time.

The Sheikh hasn't moved. Melody sees me looking. He beckons me and I follow, a lame, incontinent fool.

Melody has stuck a knife into the big guy, right into his big Sheikh heart. Jack nasty Melody has jammed that knife in and worked it around like a gearstick, twisted it like a door handle. Rich white is now rich red. His robe is blotting paper for this evil fucking crime. He's still got his shades on, still got his big face to the sun. He looks like he'll start laughing any second.

I think how Jack the bastard Melody has killed this superb man.

I don't feel anything as this killer takes my hand, as he brings it to that dagger. I watch as he wraps my empty fingers around it, presses them in and pulls away.

My hand slides off the knife, falls back to my side like its dead.

I look at Jack hate Melody and say, 'You're a prick, Jack. A real prick, you know that?'

'Yeah,' he says. 'Coming from you, that means nothing.'

I have a big attack of the blues.

He makes me get down on my knees. My heart isn't even beating now. I just want to sleep or die, whatever comes first. I can't look at Crystal and I know she can't look at me.

He calls the other two up from the face-down and we kneel, like stupid pins again, facing each other like in some ludicrous game. I can barely lift this arm now, half raising it.

Melody waves a finger at Ratface. He says, 'What is with you and this asshole Forley?

'I mean, that Bullfight performance was a joke, right? I mean, we all know that Baker "the Reactor" Forley might as well have took a shit on the damn table for all the success he took away from that, right?'

I reckon I'm open to this sewed-up moron's views on it.

I'm not sure I have any value in this world, to be honest.

Melody goes, 'I mean, you pluck this guy from some Irish potato field, some guy who's drunken dad has just killed himself, and you fill him with alcohol, tell him he can win the world championship, train him up and then drop him into live games.

'I mean, talk about a guy needing to fill a hole in his life, for Christ sakes. I mean, what did you see in him? I mean, what did you expect when you launched him into the circuit? I mean, what actually happened?

'SHIT happened! That's what. And the funniest thing about all of it, Ratface, you fuck, is that this freckle-faced loser is now your ONLY freaking client. I mean, you were someone in this dumb game, man. I mean, where did your ambition . . .'

'Hey Jack,' says Ratface, nice and slow, 'we got your texts, man.'

Melody chuckles, 'Yeah, I bet you did. So you like them? They freak you out a little, Baker?'

I say, 'Not really, to be honest.'

Ratface goes, 'They were very you, Jack. Very Jack Melody. They were all anonymous, timid, all easy route stuff. They're like you and your plan right now, this bullshit plan to, let me see now . . . kill some sinkers, steal someone else's money, bail out of the sport.

'They're like you running a knife into the big Sheikh when he's sleeping.

'They're like you when you backed out of our plan to make some money . . .'

Melody goes, 'You fucked that up, Ratface.'

'No, I showed up. I forgave and showed up. We could have done it, we could have made it, no one would have got hurt. But you didn't have the balls, Jack. You couldn't face me just because you knew I was angry.

'What it comes down to is you're a coward. You're scared of the world. You're scared of the future, you're scared you can't cope if things don't work for you.

'You're scared if you fuck some shit up that you will have to live with the fall-out from it.

'Scared of living, Jack.

'It's like you and that big Californian face of yours, Jack, implanted onto your damn yellow-bellied bones.'

Jack picks at a tooth, looks at what ends up on his nail.

Ratface goes, 'You see, a man like Baker is my gamble on the future. Things might have worked out for me and him, they might not. But I've got the balls to take a chance.

'I'll tell you about Baker, Jack. He's got guts. He needed a break in life, he came with his guts in his hands and offered them to me.

'And damn it, after the shit I went through with you, Jack, I needed someone with some ambition, with the steel in their blood to back it up.

'All you will end up with is another man's girl, another man's money.

'And sooner or later she will hate you, Jack. Everyone does. It's because you're weak, afraid, lily-livered, half-alive.

'Truth is you ain't one piece of the man Baker Forley is and you ain't ever going to be so.

'So you just keep tricking and cheating and texting, Jack. You just keep going. Whatever it is makes you feel like you're a real man, you keep doing it.

'It's all you got, Jack. It's all you got, man.'

A slow, full breeze sashays along the roof of the mad house.

I'm thinking I'm going to cry. I get that fizzy feeling behind my eyes and think maybe some little beer tears are going to come rolling out.

I feel myself taking a deep breath.

I feel kind of high.

I smile at everything in front of me.

That little tear comes, just one. It runs down my face and gets embraced and lifted away, slowly, softly, by the sun.

Ratface flicks his eyes to me, nods, then away.

I'm indebted to this man, this odd wee terrier, this shallow little hero, this bold wee legend.

Jack Melody looks at me, 'Does he grab your ass a lot, Baker?'

'Yeah,' I say, 'he keeps mistaking it for your face.'

Ratface laughs, 'That's it, man. That's why I want to slap that ass.'

I look over at him.

He stops laughing.

'I don't want to slap your ass, Baker. I don't know where I was going with tha—'

Nap says, 'Gentlemens. We have two good dead friends here so please some respect. And Mr ass Melody, kindly explain what in name fuck is happening?'

Crystal walks into view from behind. She's looking at me now, but shades on. I don't know for sure, but I might be looking at a tear under the edge of one of those big Hollywood panes.

I look away. I can't take the thought of her at this moment.

I say to Nap and Ratface, 'Well, if we're getting back to this bull-shit, I want to be clear I'm not punching anyone.'

'Yes you are you dumb potato,' says Melody.

'No I'm not, you shameless fucker,' I say. 'Jack asshole Melody.'

Melody laughs. 'I'm enjoying this weird love-hate fest guys, but seriously, can you focus on yourselves for a minute?'

Ratface says, 'We all on the same page guys? Right? We all know Melody and this evil bitch's plan, right?'

We're all silent.

Me and Nap look at each other, trying to work it out.

Brains whirr.

We're wondering if Ratface has got it all sussed.

Melody watches us.

It's like he's waiting for us to catch up.

I give up, not caring, and drift into a short violent fantasy about tricking Jack Melody into coming to Derry for a pint of getting-your-head-kicked-in.

I see him, in my mind, squaring up to some of the maddest bastards on earth, and smile to myself as they rip his plastic face off, take a shite in it and sent it floating down the Foyle.

I laugh out loud now and everyone thinks I've worked out the plan, but I'm too deeply blocked.

'Wait,' says Nap. 'Plastic Jack trying to steal from the house?'

'Not exactly,' says Ratface. 'He and Crystal are a couple, right? He's doing this with her, right? We're being set up, right? She's going to get Sheikh Alam's fortune, right?'

We say nothing.

'Ah come on guys,' says Ratface, 'it's pretty fucking straightforward.'

He shakes his head.

Melody laughs.

Ratface and Melody share a laugh.

'You see,' says Melody, 'you two guys aren't strategists. Ratface is a strategist, he can see a plan.'

Awkward silence.

Ratface doesn't look at Melody.

'Wow,' I say. It hits me. 'Yeah, that's fucking it.'

Nap's looking bothered, 'Mr Melody is doing with Lady Crystal?'

'Yeah,' says Ratface, 'obviously. Okay, so look at it this way: crazy, boozy billionaire Sheikh invites scumbag hard drinkers to his house, they drink like maniacs for three days, they go insane, have a fight, some die, wife inherits. She's to be the only witness, guys.

'Melody is obviously fucking Crystal with whatever kind of man-made dick he has.

'He has been at every competition she's been at and the two have got a thing going and hatched this nasty little plot.

'And who won't believe her story about the terrible thing that happened here? Pro drinkers are the bad guys, worldwide. Remember.'

Melody's reaching into his back pocket, 'Pro drinking is finished,' he says. He holds up his phone to show us the screen, smirks over our shoulders at Crystal. It's too bright, none of us can see it right.

Then we hear it, 'Uh, uh, uh . . . Jack . . . uh, uh . . .'

'What the hell is that?' says Ratface, squinting.

Melody says, 'That, my friend, is me fucking Crystal in that outstanding Islamic outfit.'

'Stop it Jack,' she says. 'Wise up.'

Nap's gob drops open.

'Now, now,' Melody says to him, putting away the phone. 'You didn't like that did you, little Arab? Hmm?'

The seconds of silence are sore, angry, full of aggro.

'So what's your role, Melody?' I say. 'You complete wanker.'

'My job is just to set up this stage, to kill you guys,' he says. 'But other than that, I was never here. Simple fact is Crystal came onto the roof to say goodnight, found her husband dead and Forley standing, drunk off his stupid ass. Forley grabs her, attacks her, mercilessly.

'He finishes, stands up, turns his back. She gets all fired up and runs him off the roof.

'So basically you fell off too early, Forley. Next time, it'll kill you.'

Ratface goes, 'What do you mean, attacks her?'

Melody points at the floor.

'I mean your dumb prodigy got jiggy with her, right here, before she pushed him off the roof. It got evil up here, you see. And we already got the DNA to prove the rape.'

Ratface turns to me. 'Explain that last bit,' he says. 'Is ass face saying he has a sperm sample of yours?'

I shrug.

'Explain that bit, Baker,' says Ratface. 'Why does Jack Melody have some of your junk?'

'Okay,' I say. 'There was a release, but it wasn't with—'

'DID YOU AND JACK MELODY HAVE A THING?'

'No, Jesus, no, no. I had a thing with Crystal. Jesus, calm down.'

'Oh, okay,' says Ratface. 'A what kind of thing.'

Nap's getting more and more prickly the longer this goes on. He's like Pavlov's dog, can't help himself when his brain dings, once again, to the likely realisation the Sheikh's wife has graced, faced and placed a fair few cocks. He's busting to belt someone.

Ratface repeats, 'What kind of thing?'

Melody butts in, 'Does it matter?'

'Shut up Melody,' and Ratface turns to me again. 'The shit that has been going on behind my back, I need to know – what kind of thing?'

'Just a, well, not a fuck.'

'Then what? Tantric fucking sex?'

'None of your business is what it was.'

'Yeah, it actually is my business!'

'No it isn't!'

'Baker, you're a freaking ass.'

Melody butts in, 'Guys, guys. Quit it, please, I'm laughing here.'

I have to ask, 'So what do you get out of all this, Melody?'

'I get the girl. The girl who had the brains to get the Sheikh to do this whole damn thing. The girl I been dating for the last year, the girl who has cleverly hired and worked those loyal servants at the security gate. I get the smart, lovely and soon to be unbelievably rich Crystal.'

'Lucky you,' I say. 'And I actually mean that, so I do.'

'Thanks Baker,' he says. 'I get to tell the story too. Exclusive access to the only survivor, the lady herself. The book alone should do pretty good, don't you think?'

'That figures,' says Ratface.

Melody nods, 'It does. That was our plan at one time, wasn't it? A book about an incredible happening, wasn't that it, Francisco?'

'Yeah,' nods Ratface. 'Shame you chickened out.'

'Hey, see our friend Mr Nine Hearts over there?' I say. 'One of the guys you murdered? He has an idea for a book.'

'That's right,' Ratface nods. 'A good one too.'

Nap nods now, untroubled by the violence, his face bloody.

He says, 'It's attractive story about three smart mens. The old men and the little Columbo man from Korea. It very interesting.'

And he is moving, slowly, somewhere. His little knees are, slowly, reversing away.

'Aye,' I say. 'I like the part about the guy having a wank over the flamingos.'

'Love that part,' Ratface says.

'Forley,' Melody says, 'punch Ratface.'

I say, 'Just before I do that . . .'

Nap's hand drops. He seizes the Jesus bucket, hurls it into the air. His boke takes wind like ectoplasm, splattering Crystal and Melody.

That little guy is on his feet so fast it's a blur.

I go for the bat, arm aching, and wrench it from Melody.

Nap goes for his head. He punches that prick in the centre of his ass face like a tomahawk missile.

I pull the bat from him and swing it, cracking it onto his shins.

I turn and Crystal's gathering phones, dropping one.

I run, slip right in the jesus, land on my broken arm. It hurts like nothing I ever felt before. Terrifying pain kicks through me.

I scream, like I never screamed before.

Crystal makes for the door, arms loaded with mobiles.

Ratface takes off after her. She flings the phones through, pulls it behind. It slams, locks, bolts.

It's a door we'll never break.

And we're trapped up here.

'Shite', I say, heart walloping. 'What'll happen?'

Nap must know.

'No peoples know about us up here, only Crystal and Melody. But . . .'

'Security?'

'Yes, her two mens at the gate . . .'

We all look at each other, around the roof, over the land.

We're looking for an idea.

Crystal's feet on the courtyard below. She gets into the car. We call to her, we say how she might get out of this clean.

'Baby!' I shout, as Nap and Ratface glare.

Without even looking up, she grinds the Merc's wheels into the bricks and takes off, ripping over velvet grass towards the gatehouse.

'Shite it', Nap says. 'They have the guns and do of whatever she saying.'

Ratface looks at me. I can tell he wants to say something like 'this is the worst moment of my life' or some balls, but he stays silent.

We both look at Nap. He's sucking on a fat little finger, biting it, thinking. He takes it from his mouth and points it into the air. Ratface and I look up.

'Gaudí's grave,' he says.

I say, 'Wha?'

'The grave. Mr Gaudí's grave, under the house.'

He points down.

We look.

He points out over the house.

I'm all, 'Oh Jesus wept. What? Jump? I can't do that.'

'No, no, you potato,' Nap's shaking his hand in my face. 'The pool.'

He leads us to a far corner.

Nap points down.

Yes. The pool. The pool that looks like you're looking down on naked people in the pool.

No.

It's too far.

'We wouldn't make it,' I say. 'It's too far. We'd land on the cement.'

Nap points along the roof, to where it bows down, as if melted by the sun. 'If we run this down fast,' he says, 'we can jump at the end and we will make it.'

I go, 'Ah fuck's sake, hey.'

Ratface shakes his head. 'Come on Baker, you freaking Irish wuss.'

I go, 'My arm's broke, my ribs are mashed up and I'm about ninety percent alcohol. Fuck you.'

'Your arm? Your drinking arm?'

'Yes, my drinking arm.'

'Christ Baker, you jerk, I couldn't trust you with a damn onion.'

'Right, cheers.'

'And you pissed yourself too. I didn't like to say earlier.'

'Yeah, I knew that. A guy knows when he's fricking satchelled, cheers.'

Nap's looking over the roof, checking the angle.

'Gentlemens,' he says, 'straight down, this slope.'

I say, 'At fifty fucking miles per hour hitting water or concrete are much the same thing, you know. Even if we make it we'll probably die. Just so you know, like.'

Nap just goes right ahead. He climbs over the little wall, edges to where the slope begins, gets into a running stance and says, 'I see you at the pool. We only have moments, gentlemens.'

He takes a step, then breaks into a run. His little legs blur and he takes a breath as he belts off like a ground-bound rocket along the tiles.

We stare, agog, as he shoots off the edge, wriggling his limbs into the air, and just makes it to the blinking blue water. He slams in, tilted backwards, still running.

The whole mad thing took about one second.

We both stare down. He has stopped. There is no movement. There's silence.

His little body, now a black and white blob in the water, appears to have ceased living.

I say, 'He's dead.'

'He ain't dead you damn pessimist, Baker.'

'Well he's underwater and he's not moving.'

'He's taking a rest. That's been a shock to the guy after all that gin and shit, and his boss getting killed and shit. Here – give me a hand with Melody.'

Ratface is pacing towards Jack Melody.

I don't know why.

He grabs at his feet, wants me to help lift him. He's still out cold.

I look, 'Why? To do what? There's no time.'

Ratface looks at me like I'm stupid. 'Baker, you know the way you're like eighty percent dense?'

'No.'

'Well this is the densest moment of your life. I am not, repeat not, letting this asshole walk away from this.'

'So we're going to throw him off the roof? That's the brainwave? A simple murder?'

'No. I'm going to blow him into the sky. A fucking brilliant murder.'

Fuck yes.

I go, 'Great idea.'

'Glad you got there. Now, careful with that arm and . . . lift . . .'

We stick Melody onto the pod, onto the pouting mouth of the fountain, face up. One of his fake teeth has broken. He groans a little as Ratface rifles his pockets, takes a wallet, a phone.

From below, 'Hurry up you damns.'

I peer over.

Nap's standing, soaked, blinking into the sun, wiping his face, waving. 'I hear them coming.'

We make sure Melody's going to get it point blank.

We nod at each other.

'It's a fine thing we do, Baker,' he says.

'Too fucking right.'

I wonder what it was that made Melody not turn up that night.

I wonder what broke these two guys up so savagely.

For all of Ratface's bravado, he ultimately isn't keen on this next move. Nor am I. He tells me the only way down for him is to hold my hand.

'To hold my hand?'

'Come on Baker, you won't save a friend's life?'

'A friend's life? I need my hands and arms and shit to run and land properly. I'm not—'

'Look, you're goddamn blocked out of your box much more than me. The booze takes pain away so when it comes to landing, you're actually the lucky one here.'

I feel like decking the bastard.

Nap starts jumping up and down. 'You assholes!'

We go for it. Ratface grips my right hand like some kind of animal bite.

'Ahhhh, that hurts . . .'

We step out, make our way a few feet along the ledge to the slope like scared children. We get onto it, get into running poses, holding hands, and he puts a foot forward by mistake. And we're taken by gravity.

In half a second we're belting, then falling, then crashing into each other, then breaking into some kind of roll, a crocodile still clamped to me.

I get a punch in the face.

I catch a fearful, yellowed-eye.

We hit clean, light, empty air.

We zoom into a breeze.

I close my eyes.

I hear, 'You freakin . . . !'

And then a gunshot.

Chapter Nineteen

My dad went that way, flying into the air.

He went flying in a car, landed on water, sank slow, died hard.

He sat in that car, his shirt and tie on, his seat belt on, and let Lough Swilly rage and roar in through the open windows.

He did suicide with dignity, with an unbending will, pissed out of his head on the poteen some client had tipped him with.

Too much pro bono.

He gave too much of himself, too much sacrifice in return for being able to feel he had done the right thing. So much right thing that it made him hated and depressed when he tried to call time, when he tried to say no. He was fleeced and finished by his own free goodness.

Flying into that water was meant to make things easier for us, his last sacrifice, his bad path to getting us his life insurance. But it was too simply clear that he'd necked that shitty liquor and killed himself, and the company guys called in person with lock, stock and barrel documents to say, 'You've no chance.'

All too weird.

Part of me always admired him for it, admired that he had tough, good guts.

But most of me, at one time or another, hated those guts.

Jason Johnson

He left us nothing but debt and door knocks from broke political clowns and three street soldiers.

I think about his face now, about how he was such a good swimmer, how he could slice through the waves like a razor blade.

I think about my face, my blunted life and hear myself saying I've no right to question anything he did.

If one of us deserved heaven . . .

I come round, getting dragged from the nudie pool by two small, wet men.

My arm pumps in agony as it's tugged.

Barbed wire is being yanked through my mind.

I try to engage the legs but they're too light, or too heavy, to operate.

They talk fast as they drop me on cement, grabbing my feet now.

My head starts bumping along bricks.

I see in my head that I'm leaving a big slug trail of pool water and, probably, worse.

We get to a big brown wooden side door as I'm trying to say, 'Please just stop . . .'

A bullet cracks its frame, a little army of splinters in all directions, as Nap pulls me the last of the way through.

He slams the door, locks it, ducks down.

Ratface is already inside, arse on the floor, rubbing his face with a shaking hand. One of his shoulders is banjaxed, jammed upwards. You could hang a coat off it.

When the ache stops for half a second, the first thing I feel is annoyed.

Another bullet pounds, sounds like it might have torn through the door.

I look to see if anyone's dead.

They aren't.

I lean on a cupboard, try to pull myself up.

A shot slams through the window, into the wall behind, a vicious battalion of glass splinters in its wake.

These guys are crazy, shooting all over, untrained, off their heads, hell-bent on bagging us for her.

I might jesus.

Nap takes the lead, points, dashes off, his head down. Slowly, we start. Slowly we begin the walking that we urgently need to make into a dash through the house of fun.

There's door after door after door, big walls, small walls, wood, smells and pictures.

Ratface, behind me, hits the words hard, 'Nap, start the damn fountain.'

Nap goes, 'Please again?'

I find voice. I have to insist.

I say, 'Start it, Nap.'

Nap stops, turns round. He looks at me, my head pounding so bad it's making me blink in rhythm, my arm hanging like dead meat

My eyes twist.

Nap looks at me like he's sorry, like I'm fading away.

Yet he's a little angry.

He says, 'Why the all of hell you want—'

'Start the damn fountain, Nap,' says Ratface.

Nap waves a little hard fist in the air, he can't find words.

We stare.

I say, 'Do it. Just do it.'

'You beering fucks.'

Off he goes, ducked and scurrying back between us, around a corner, half his normal size, twice the speed.

Ratface is breathing badly and I feel bad for a second.

He goes, 'Where did you . . . fuck Crystal?'

'Shut up.'

'No Baker,' he says. 'I mean, it's fine . . . do what you like . . .'

'Cheers.'

'. . . I just mean, where and when. How? I mean, there was no time. You've been drunk as a frickin' . . . empty glass for days.'

'Why do you need to know this crap?'

'Baker, I need to know. I just need to know things. You're the only one who can tell me, you asswipe. So pretty please. Where and when did you do it?'

I feel sorry for him.

'In the house. The first night. She came into my room.'

'I figured,' he says. 'I knew she was lurking around, eyeing herself up some red gear. What happened?'

'Not saying.'

'Blowie? Handie? Full on bouncy? What?'

'Jesus Christ. You need to know this now?'

A door opens somewhere. We both look up and down the corridor and then to each other.

No idea where we are in this impossible house.

Dogs are barking.

'A hand job, right. She must've had a test tube or something with her, to collect . . . it.'

Ratface nods. 'Where do you think it is?'

I look at him.

There's footsteps.

'Where do I think my junk is?'

He goes, 'Yeah.'

I go, 'What the fuck? Why, I mean . . . would you like to fucking *have it*? You *freak*. You want that fucking keepsake?'

'No you dickwad,' he says quietly, urgently. 'Man, you're so dumb. It's evidence, you freaking pea-brain. You need to get it before it's used against you. She can say anything about a pro drunk like you and when she brings out your muck it'll become fact. Comprende?'

I nod, 'Rightttt, I get ya.'

'For the damn record, Baker, I don't want a test tube of your fucking jizz, you freaking pervert. I worry what you take me for sometimes, you damn anus.'

The dogs.

Closer now.

We're not dealing with all this danger very well.

What do we do? We look at the doors around us. Which one?

Nap comes bolting around the corner, almost on all fours, ushering us forward with those low hands.

He goes, 'Rush, rush.'

We run hard.

'They collect dogs now bring them in house,' he says, passing between us. 'Imagine orders must kill from Lady Crystal. Run very fast gentlemens.'

We take a corner, hearts thumping, into a wider corridor, all maroon red, bad nightclub style.

Ratface says, wheezing, 'Did you . . . do the fountain?'

'Yes, I do fucking fountain, is fucking do, man. Okay!'

'Great stuff,' I say, meaning it.

He goes, 'Follow this way.'

A broad purple door. We're though it, closing it behind.

There's a corridor straight ahead, dipping down to the entrance of a wide, spiralling stairwell. Broad steps, two foot by two foot, bite their way into the earth and we run them.

We go further, it gets darker.

Down and round, round and down, on it goes.

Down.

Down.

Now the scent of old, of crusty, of mould.

Now everything is lit by ultraviolet.

'Fuck me pink, this house just goes on being insane,' I say.

Ratface, panting, agrees, 'No shit.'

Nap, breathing fast, says, 'It's excessively planned like much of Gaudí's work.'

It's hard to see where each broad step ends, where the next begins.

Ratface says, 'How damn deep does this place go?'

'Mr Gaudí said it goes all the way to his grave.'

We run onwards to his grave. In time we're getting the rhythm right, bouncing down and down and down towards some kind of deep-end death.

A minute, or minutes, or more, or less. Nothing is relative, comparable. Nothing is in context in this dead, deep, cold place.

I almost smack into Ratface's back.

'Jesus.'

His breathing is bad. I don't know if he can go on.

He says, 'What . . . are we . . . doing?'

Nap jams on his brakes, 'Why stop?'

Ratface takes a deeper breath. 'I mean, won't they . . . just

follow? I mean, don't you think the . . . dogs can catch us? I mean
. . . where are we going?'

It's a good question.

And if these steps go all the way to a grave, then why are we
running anyway? What good is a grave to us? Seems a bit one-way
to my mind.

'Nap,' I say. 'What's this Gaudí grave shite? I mean, what's down
here? And anyway, I need to get that semen sample of mine. It's
got to be in the house somewhere.'

I can barely make out Nap ahead of me now. But he's definitely
there, the frustrated total silence working as some kind of proof.

His teeth flash in the black light. 'I sorry, semen sample? Like
from perhaps cow?'

'A bull, aye. Because Crystal wanked me off and took the
stuff . . .'

'HEY! You no tell me that!'

I can see him clench those square little gnashers.

Silence.

I say, 'Sorry.'

Ratface says, 'Nap, we just need to know where . . .'

'HEY RATFACE AND MR REACTOR. No, no, no. I not help.
If you say once more about dirt with Sheikh Alam's wife then I will
kick box you in the face all the way into grave. Okay? You understand that you moron bastards?'

Silence.

'Now gentlemens,' he says. 'If you go back up the two men and
two dogs will kill you, I promise that with my heart. And they will
kill me. I promise it. They are hired crazies, old jail-mad crazies,
spend their day on drugs and *Grand Theft Auto*, they love to shoot
and shoot and do any exact detail the Lady Crystal will tell them.

Believe me. Semen sample is not the big problem. Perhaps Crystal will maybe have the disgust of thing with her anyway.'

'Yeah,' I say. 'Let's forget it.'

'Okay,' says Ratface, a flash of the rodent-like teeth. 'Okay, your call, Baker. So what now? We can't go up. What happens if we go down? Won't they just follow?'

'Gentlemens, you can stupid and stand here like the breasts for the rest of time if you choose to be standing so, or you can come with me. But I am going at this point. Trust me gentlemens, you have made for me to say that time is at the short.'

He goes.

I hear his little feet move on, tap, tap, tapping downwards into the UV blackness.

Ratface and me just stand there on those giant steps, being dumb, at least 80 percent dumb.

My arm hurts like fuck.

I say, 'If you said to me now you could cut my arm off and it would stop this pain I'd probably go with it.'

Ratface goes, 'Yeah, relevant point, well made. Cut your drinking arm off. This is just the place to decide and then execute that little bit of insanity, you freaking cabbage. You know Baker, you never cease to amaze me with your stupidness and tragedies.'

I say, 'Away back to your caravan, you oul fucking prune.'

Behind us, above us, something moves. It's a faint rustle, like paper lifted by wind, but it's a sign we should be doing something other than what we are doing.

Ratface says, 'I guess we just have to go see the late Mr Gaudí, Baker.'

'I think we should.'

The UV fades as we go, the reach of the electricity gone. It soon leaves us in pure, ink black. We get that good pace again – two steps, drop – two steps, drop – on and on and on. I don't know what kind of distance we are covering or how far down this corkscrew into the world we've travelled. Time is all lost and getting more lost in this demented house's massive arsehole.

Ratface, wheezing, says, bit by bit, 'So you . . . think . . . Gaudí's . . . grave is . . . really here?'

'How the fuck would . . . I know?'

'I'm pretty sure . . . he's . . . buried under the Sagrada . . . Familia.'

'Whatever . . . I haven't . . . a baldy.'

'That would be . . . too weird, if we found . . . Gaudí's grave.'

'Yeah.'

He goes, 'You . . . think . . . your Crystal baby has . . . the security guys . . . wrapped around . . . her . . . finger . . . because . . . she is fucking . . . them . . . as well . . . ?'

I go, 'Yeah, which makes you . . . the only man alive left with zero sex life.'

He's all, 'Hey dickwad . . . you have . . . NO . . . idea . . . about my . . . private . . .'

I stop. 'Hey.'

Ratface stops. '. . . life. What?'

'Where the fuck's Nap?'

We both listen. No longer any sound from below.

'Hey – Nap?' I kind of whisper a shout.

Ratface is louder, 'Nap? You there?'

I can't hear anything from anywhere. It's like we're stuck now, nowhere, in the middle of zero, dark as the inside of a horse, right on the edge of some sort of hell.

'Baker.'

'Yeah.'

'If this is . . . it. I mean . . . if this is . . . where it ends . . .'

'Wise up, there's . . . a way out of this.'

'I just wanted to say if this is where . . . it ends, if there isn't a way out, I wanted to say that . . . I think you're an awesome sinker, that it's been a pleasure . . . working with you.'

'Yeah, you too. I appreciate all you've done for me, all you said back there about me. You're a gentleman, so you are.'

I can feel him, reaching out in the dark, trying to get an arm around me, good and low, trying to touch my arse.

I move away. He flails around for a minute, almost falls.

'Let's just go, right?'

'Yeah. Okay. Fuck it.'

I say, 'Hey, before you go. I got to ask it . . . why did Melody not show that time you had the scam all arranged? Why did you two guys fall out?'

He goes, 'Oh man. You pick your moments. Truth is, Baker, the damn freak . . . that asshole . . . called me that thing, he called me Ratface. Right to my face. And I'm exceptionally . . . sensitive about that shit, as you know.

'He called me Ratface, we had a fight, I smashed his face up as a kind of return of the . . . insult and, as it goes, he was . . . too damn vain and embarrassed to go anywhere after that.

'He collapsed the whole . . . house of cards over it, man. He brought it down because he was too embarrassed about the face I gave him. I mean, what a prick, right?'

I say, 'Right, well . . .'

'Guy got totally fucked addicted . . . to plastic surgery after that. I mean, what a vain asshole, right?'

I go, 'Yeah.'

He says, 'Cool. Appreciate your support. I'm going now, okay?'

I go, 'Okay. Good luck.'

He goes.

Two more steps.

And he's gone.

It's amazing. I hear him grunt, like he's clearing his throat, and then I feel a cold wind on my face.

I feel him vanish from the world.

'Er . . . Rat—?'

Nothing.

'Francisco? You disappear?'

Zilch.

'Oh balls.'

I have to keep going, to find out what happened, to see if I evaporate too, to see if I become suddenly nothing, to see where and what and how.

'Fuck it.'

There's a distant crash, some kind of splash, or smash, or collision. It's a kind of plop, a drop, a dump, a watery slap. It could be the sound of life or death.

I say, 'Dear God. It's maybe a wee bit late in the day and all, but cheers for the talent . . .'

I've got one hand, a karate chop prayer, the other arm too sore to lift.

'. . . and sorry for all the shite. Amen.'

I walk onto the next step.

'Okay my main man, keep 'er lit . . .'

And onto the next.

Chapter Twenty

We'd heard that fountain load itself with those thousands of gallons of water before it blasted Jack Melody into the heavens.

It took it just a few high-volume seconds to suck up the whole river flowing under the Gaudí house. It was drawn skywards through a whirring, clicking and creaking piping system, locked firm at the top of the property and then, after a heavily pregnant pause, hosed out like a colossal act of nature.

The three of us had been struggling around in the water in the dark, wondering if we were alive or dead or dying until that engine fired up. We heard the massive mechanical inhale and the level plunged like someone pulled a plug. We ended up sitting on the riverbed, soaking wet, amazed, stumped, stupid.

The falling was sensational. It was a free drop for what felt like ages, then it was like being hit over and over in a pillow fight, then it was diving into freezing cold water.

I'd bit my tongue, yelped, been winded, dead-legged and whiplashed, but hitting the water, sinking and coming up for air for the second time in those few mad hours was strange, sweet, cleansing, sobering relief all the same.

The machine moaned and the river vanished around us and Nap said to stand up and make our way towards the light beaming in from gaps in the rocks ahead.

As my vision cleared, I could see we were in a giant cave, like something out of Batman. I could feel it was cold and stale and, above, I could see a red haze, as if the high walls were glowing.

Nap followed my eyes and smiled. He said it was wine, tens of thousands of unreachable bottles of wine in the deepest, biggest, greatest, grandest cellar on earth.

'They call it Gaudí's grave,' he said. 'They build it so amazing and put all the wine in. It's why Sheikh Alam buy the house.'

Ratface was utterly dumbfounded.

'But how could you even . . . get to it?' he asked, straining his neck, turning around and around. 'I mean . . . the wine is . . .'

'It collapse,' said Nap. 'The cellar built, the wine was put in, then they put later the big fountain in and it all go wrong. It collapse. The stairs collapse. The floor fall away in the river. The cellar entire now just hangs in the air, stopped in time, this such lovely red glow, forever. It is priceless. You can't get the wine, gentlemens.'

He said the Sheikh was considering rebuilding the cellar, but hadn't committed to losing his privacy, to allowing others to find out the truth about the local rumour, about this great, old, deep secret.

'But one day near the death I know true he did want to get the cellar made again,' said Nap, 'and then he was going to drink his face removed off, drink the old wines Gaudí and Dalí had knew of and sing in the echoes until dead.

'I know the thinking made him happy. I think maybe he wanted a man such as liking you Mr Forley for his big pissing-up session with the forever wine.'

We all drank in that elegant shading, those deep, mosaic curtains on those blood-black walls.

Said Nap, 'Sheikh Alam had big, softie cushions purchased, hanging from roof from where once steps appeared. You can see straight above heads. Those are what breaks your falls, gentlemens. They guide you downwards.

'He liked to jump into the water sometimes with no clothings around his personal body and say his cheers and think about all the wine ocean. It was his happiness.

'I knew today we would not be killed too much if we jumped, but I knew there was only minutes until the fountain loaded.'

We looked directly up, a white, soft, swinging chandelier emerging from the darkness.

I started wondering if the men were still chasing us. We all wondered if they would come suddenly falling down, flying and flapping with skydiving dogs at their sides, bashing the cushions, only to land on what was now a riverbed with no river.

It would be fatal.

We all shrugged and moved on towards the light.

We found ourselves climbing up rocks and out into the bright Spanish day.

We walked, lightheaded, heavy footed, into a big green sunny field, an enormous, sprawling, glorious vineyard, the lapping, radiant Mediterranean spread out forever and breathing in the distance.

Water began gurgling and flowing back to where we had been as we found straight, solid ground and fell, wet and drying, onto the cool, rich grass.

'It's beautiful,' I said, on the edge of a faint, my arm broken in more places than I could count, my heart beating and buzzing with some kind of sudden happiness.

The second last thing I heard was Ratface groaning, 'Oh man, can someone get me a freaking ambulance.'

The last thing I heard was some kind of scream, some sort of howl, from somewhere inside what we had left.

Chapter Twenty-One

I am so comfortable I feel like crying.

I am balled up, foetal, in the darkness, in a box, in the corner, for hours, and it is about the most sumptuous, private nothing I've ever done.

I cannot feel now the momentous thirst, the agonising arm, the sweat or the might of the buckling heat pushing its way through everything to eat at me.

I am still and unstressed.

I'm not consuming, barely thinking, not caring.

I have no comfort zone to leave in this world, only comfort zones to find.

If I survive this empty joy, if I make it to the mainland, if I stay out of jail, I'm going to start experimenting with sensory deprivation. I'll buy a little wooden box, bury it deep down and far in the country somewhere, live in it in a state of bliss, until I blindly, happily die off.

Maybe I am already dying. Maybe this is what you do.

There might be that tunnel coming up.

The only sound now is the slow, safe, womby drone of the engine coming at me, purring, from all directions.

I don't know where I am, can't tell if my eyes are open or closed . . .

We had made it to the marina. We had walked, winding and falling our way through vines, to make it to the side of the road, where we collapsed and cowered, all burning and quiet and ready to quit.

Nap watched the road, keeping an eye out for traffic heading to and from the Gaudí house, to see if he could get a sense of how much shit we were in, of how badly and deeply we had been framed.

'Clear out Nap,' I said. 'You've helped us enough. Go back, tell them this has nothing to do with you.'

'Bullshit, Mr Forley,' he said. 'Lady Crystal is wanting us all dead and her word is boss. Believe please, those drugs and games two mens will kill me before I can speak words. Don't you see she told them we killed Sheikh Alam so they now will be killing all around?'

I said, 'But those guys . . . I mean . . . maybe they're . . . ah balls, I don't know.'

I didn't know what I knew anymore.

I lay back, shutting up, putting my head in the Spanish grass and watched a shining beetle watch me.

'Hey, Baker,' said Ratface. 'Fuck you. Let Nap deal with this. You keep staring at the ground, you damn tomato.'

Nap stayed silent. And then, 'I think maybe it's true, they are dead mens. Maybe two and the dogs, maybe they fell far and hard. Or maybe one is not fall when other fall.'

In fairness to Nap, random guessing did seem to be the best way of getting any information at this stage.

He said, 'But I think maybe she will call for the more insane security and at one point the police.'

I thought how the beetle, by then climbing onto some animal

shit, still eyeing me as potential competition for the turd, had a simpler and nobler life than me.

Ratface tinkered with Melody's phone but got nowhere. It was password protected and twice dumped deep in water, so it was basically about as useful as a top-of-the-range photocopier right now.

He cursed at it, hit it off a stone, whispered viciously at it and came close to biting it before looking at me as if to say 'this is the worst damn phone situation of all time' and chucking it into some vines.

I'd no idea who he was even planning to call, and he probably didn't either.

Nap suddenly stood up and waved at a car, at a local cab driver who did some work for the Sheikh.

The guy pulled over at the side of the road in the small SEAT, clearly knowing nothing of what had been going on. As we gathered ourselves, dashed over and got in, I'm sure I heard the distant rush of a fountain.

Nap started a Spanish conversation as a bottle of water was passed around. I cranked my neck to see if Jack Melody has taken to the sky, but could see nothing.

Ratface was perched too close to me for comfort in that car, tragically the smallest taxi on the island.

His breath was like something out of *Alien*.

'You don't look good, man,' he said, point blank.

'I don't feel the very best, to be honest.'

'You look even more sunburned now as well. You might need a doctor.'

'Can you turn your head slightly away please,' I said. 'Your breath fucking stinks like dead sheep.'

'Fuck you, man. I'm just conversing. This is the maddest day of all time, I spent it with you, I thought I might just . . .'

'Turn away now or I swear I'll fucking rip your tongue out in the back of this car and throw it out the window.'

'So you've finally gone insane, Baker. Besides, you've only got one arm with a complete fricking bone in it and I'm not going to let you do any more damage . . .'

There was about twenty-five seconds of mayhem. I shoved Ratface into the door with my dead, floppy arm, head-butted the side of his face, stuck my fingers into his mouth, grabbed what I could.

He bit back hard, chewing while forcing me away with his pointy little shoulder. He did some kind of animalistic spitting thing as I tried to get the tongue.

Nap was shouting, 'Gentlemens, gentlemens!' but it was no good. He told the guy to pull over just as I got Ratface's fetid flesh nipped.

He sank teeth deep into one of my fingers, catching right between a knuckle. I yelled and pulled that slithering old ming, swearing an oath to god almighty that I would rip the fucking thing off.

The door opened and Ratface fell back, my digits still clamped on his foul, greasy, stinking whip.

'Gentlemens!' said Nap, catching him. 'No violence in the SEAT please, please, please.'

I knew when I saw Nap curl a fist that I had to let go or I'd get knocked out.

The beauty was Ratface found it hard to speak afterwards, although I know he wanted to say some offensive shite about me.

We drove onwards to the marina in silence, the driver checking us both in the mirror, worried about the smelly, violent bastards in the back of his car, worried about what exactly he had got caught up in.

The guy called it quits, gave Nap his phone as part of some deal and dropped us off near a couple of parked-up articulated trucks within sight of Sheikh Alam's big yacht.

We sneaked between them, then quietly underneath, to get a decent view, to see if there was any activity around it.

'I can get yacht spare keys from marina office,' said Nap, 'but maybe police are watching, or maybe some of these security maniacs are watching.'

So we waited a while, trying not to lose focus, trying to stay alert enough in case the beer-laden truck above us started up and drove off, leaving us like guts with shirts on.

Nap said nothing when he made his move. He just moved out, leaving Ratface and me lying there, half alive.

'Am haff duhed,' said Ratface, his tongue cut, swollen in his rotted, dank cave of a mouth.

'You're half deaf?'

He held a knackered hand to his head, pistol-style, and shot himself.

'Right,' I said. 'You're half dead. Me too. Won't be long for the other half now.'

He said nothing else.

Despite the positioning making it easily possible, there was no hand on the arse.

Nap arrived back having darted to the marina office.

'Coast is very clear,' he said, opening his hand, flashing a set of keys. 'We take *The Sand Bed*, okay?'

'Jesus, yes,' I said. 'Sounds like luxury to me. Hope there's some painkillers on board.'

Ratface agreed, adding, 'Splanesh muhinund hur ee kom.'

We hadn't noticed the speedboat slowly circling the marina, its three bullet-headed men in black.

The drone of the engine is somehow connected with my heartbeat and it makes me think of a song I know from somewhere.

I step away from my mind, let it find the music, let it play the tune to me, unaided, unforced.

Nap's new phone rings – brutally – to the tune of 'Ravel's Bolero' and I think how it's at this moment the tune I hate most in the world, my all-time least liked number.

I feel like saying that to Ratface, thinking how he would like to know that detailed, irrelevant shite.

'*Sí*,' Nap whispers now from the box beside me. 'No? Okay. *Sí, gracias por su gentileza.*'

I don't know and I don't care.

'Gentlemens?'

Ratface's box is on the other side of Nap's, furthest away from me. There's no sound.

There's a pause.

So I say, 'What is it Nap?'

'My friend in marina calls. He can see the men in the black circling yacht have followed and now pulled up beside.'

'Okay,' I say, still tuned to the droning, still looking for that song.

'He says now . . . they getting on the yacht.'

'Okay,' I say.

'He say they . . . have guns.'

'Okay,' I say. 'Any word from next door?'

'What is next door?'

'The other box. From Francisco?'

'Hey,' says Nap, 'Mr Ratface Fall? Are you okay?'

Nothing.

And nothing.

I shout it, 'Hey.'

'*Shhhh*,' says Nap, 'you fool – is easy to hear.'

'I need to know my coach is okay,' I say. 'I need to know that right away.'

And nothing.

Nothing, just the drone of the engine.

'Don't die on me, coach, don't die in that box.'

And then a little, 'I'm okay man, I'm okay, no sweat, stay cool.'

And I'm glad.

'And you know you're right, man,' he says. 'I can smell my own breath in this damn cardboard cube and it's making my fricking eyes shrink.'

I smile to myself, just for a second.

I think how it's cool my mate's alive, that everything's fine, that whatever happens next will be just fine too.

And my brain tells me that tune was an old song my mum and dad used to dance to, a Duran Duran track from the eighties.

> *. . . and the sun drips down bedding heavy behind,*
> *the front of your dress all shadowy lined,*
> *the droning engine throbs in time with your beating heart . . .*

Chapter Twenty-Two

Crystal plays poker with a fluidity and ease of movement that make her more interesting than her cards, more sexy than the game.

The big ballbags around her watch, snared, as she flashes numbers and suits to herself, as she taps a painted nail on the table, as she says stop, as she asks for more, as she twists and turns.

The guys all like the deep Cleopatra eyelines and eyeshadow, the straight, hard bloody lips, the apple breasts, the brilliant, spotless white of her outfit, the way she's so fucking loaded with pull and confidence and cash she can never really lose.

They hit on her, one after the other, and get blown out or brushed off or put down or just plain ignored. She's a half-perfect slice of beguile, too cold to touch, too tepid to talk, too unique to consume.

And we don't know what to do.

'We need a plan, a strategy,' says Ratface, holding a little espresso cup, wearing Audrey Hepburn sunglasses, a pink fedora pulled down as far as it goes.

And I say, 'Do we?'

A man in a restaurant told me Crystal has been in Monte Carlo for a month. He said she arrived from Paris in a car that used to belong to one of the richest men in the world.

'But that guy got murdered,' the guy told me. 'He got stabbed to death by some drunks he brought over for a party at his house in Mallorca. A pro drinker and his coach. Real assholes, those guys.'

He says, 'One of them was an Irish guy, like you.'

'Jesus. Really?'

'Yeah. Some people are bastards, eh? It's a sport for bastards anyway.'

'Agreed.'

I told the guy I'd missed all this, that I'd been climbing Everest.

'You look it,' he said. Then, 'And they killed that PDTV guy too, you heard of him? Jack Melody?'

'Oh yeah, the guy who did reports on all the games and stuff? He was great.'

'Yeah. He was great. They killed him – nasty – and they tried to kill her too but she got away.'

'That's good to hear.'

'The drunks got away too. They've not been found yet. They forced one of the Sheikh's employees, some dumb little waiter, to take them to his yacht. He sailed them to the mainland. Sinker bastards probably dumped him in the water, poor guy.'

I said, 'Wow. Awful stuff.'

'They've never been seen since. Police reckon they probably split up. Last I heard the cops were still looking for the Irishman and a rat-faced American soak who could be anywhere. The cops say they tried to get money out of some account the Sheikh had made for them, but it got a watch put on it, they couldn't get a cent.'

'Jesus. Well, at least we know they're totally, painfully broke anyway.'

He said, 'Yeah. Let's hope it's all another nail in the coffin for that stupid sport anyway.'

I nodded deeply.

I knew this.

I knew they'd found Jack Melody in the trees getting eaten by birds and flies. Most of him anyway. I knew the power of that water jet blew his clothes off and teeth out on impact. He was spotted rocketing into the sky by some people on a plane about half a mile away.

The papers reported what they knew of the whole Gaudí house murders, said it was all drunken tragedy, all boozy terror, all the work of demons, psychos, weirdos.

Which was largely fair enough.

We found Crystal via Twitter, via tabloid, via sad pix of her all alone, the weight of the murder of her husband on her narrow shoulders, in one of the richest little cities in the world.

After climbing out of the back of that boiling articulated beer lorry we vanished in among the innards of the docks at Barcelona. We had two weeks lying low in a dirt-cheap hotel full of dealers and cockroaches before we got word and began making our way to Monte Carlo.

We weren't even sure why, but the key to getting this resolved, to lifting any murder charges or any death threats off our backs lay with Crystal.

She was the one who sent the security team and their dogs and guns to get us, to kill us, at the Gaudí house. She was the one who called in the cops and told the murderous lies about us. She was the one who had those goons patrol the marina at

Mallorca in case we made off in *The Sand Bed*.

Nap's friend had spotted the three bullet-headed heroes eyeing up the big yacht. He warned him about it just before we got on board. He saved us from being buried at sea.

Nap had sent us back under the trucks, jumped on the yacht himself steered that beauty out into the waters. He had programmed it on a course for Barcelona before slipping off the side, swimming like a hero and meeting us back at the lorry.

His courage had been immense. His deed of life-saving diversion let Crystal know we were still out there, that we were smart, and that not all of us were blocked all of the time.

Ratface nudges my slinged-up arm with his slinged-up arm.

He says, 'She knows it's us sitting here man, I'm telling you.'

'Yeah well. She's not going to say anything.'

'Hope not.'

'Nah. She's got all she wanted. Her only worry is that we collectively go and drop her name to the police, tell our story. We've got power in this game right now and she knows it. We need to make some kind of deal.'

Ratface shakes his head. 'None of that is an option. You don't get it, man. You still don't get it. All that's too risky, Baker. Remember, we are murderers, we killed Jack asshole Melody. Who's to say we didn't kill the Sheikh? Us guys?'

Nap sits up, urgently. 'That man stares at her breasts.'

I say, 'Nap, give it up. Stop working. Your boss is dead. And that heartless bitch nearly had you killed.'

He says, 'No calling bitch, Baker, please. But yes.'

Ratface says, 'We need a quality, detailed strategy, a way forward. Problem is you're damn useless with plans and shit.'

I go, 'Take it easy, all is fine. We're just a bit down on our luck, a bit skint. We'll work it out. We'll arrange something soon enough.

'Let's lie low some more, let it blow over. Relax. Everybody relax. Let's see what happens.'

Night time and Crystal knocks on my shitty hotel door in Nice.

She's got a bottle of wine in her hand and is wearing a coat that suggests, to my broken mind, she's not wearing knickers.

She goes, 'Hey stranger, fancy a nightcap?'

I go, 'Holy fuck. You recognised me?'

'Are you joking? The big ginger Irish beard, the ginger skin-head? The little rat in a pink hat sitting beside you? Nap in a flippin' St Tropez T-shirt? I haven't taken complete leave of my shagging senses, no matter what you might think.'

I look at her face and think about how much art I have seen but how little I know about it, about how much I know about beauty.

And I see suddenly a tear glitter, right in the corner of an eye, a sparkle where the black lines meet.

I'd seen one close to there before.

I think I can feel the heaviness now, the weight of her sadness.

'I wanted to say . . . my con . . .' she says, and looks down, her voice changed, instantly without glamour.

There's a pause.

I said, 'Your con?'

'My conscience,' she says, looking up, breathing in, 'is fucking hounding me to death.'

I nod.

'I don't blame it,' I say. 'You are a fucking disgrace to humanity. Come in.'

'Okay,' she says. 'Thank you, Baker.'

'Aye,' I say. 'Much to discuss.'

Epilogue

Eighteen months later and this is me, right now, playing a game with vodka number twenty-six. I'm pausing, stopping, for just one powerful second, in the sure knowledge this is the last time today the man opposite will see my full, uninterrupted face.

There's a string of Vladivar unspooling from his lip, his eyes are closing, shutting him down.

He hiccups.

I hold up the glass, pause again . . . break the chain, upset the pattern, interrupt the flow – I . . . show my control . . . I go ahead: and . . . I . . . – wait for it – sink the little clear, clean glass and fuck it over my head into the crowd.

The fans roar.

They want the glass, my shot glass.

These crazy bastards.

I get that buzz I get, maybe now the only buzz I get. I know I've done it again, that I'm walking out of here with money, with pride.

Proud of me, of my style, of my comeback.

Proud as can be in my Darby O'Kills T-shirt, my tribute to that thriving, trendy bar back in Derry (*A$$tro* can go fuck itself).

The other guy's eyes close. He starts to slide off his chair, unplugged, detached, dismissed, over and out.

The judge catches him, the medics run over, and the fans scream.

I go to stand, to suck this up, to get my hands in the air, to wave my 'I Heart Derry Very Much' cap around my head, and I can't.

I shove the chair backwards, but it was the only support I had. I fall, arse first.

It thumps the ground.

A moment later, my head thumps the ground.

The fans are going insane.

I think . . .

. . . *remember to roll* . . .

And I think . . .

. . . *DO NOT JESUS.*

Ratface is here, holding my face, looking into my eyes.

'You did it buddy,' he says, 'you did it, didn't I tell you?'

Yeah.

I'm the new London Champion. I'm king of the capital, kicking English arse across thirty-two boroughs.

I was favoured, the favourite, and I proved it.

Not a problem.

I go dizzy for a second. My eyes swivel, vision blurs, colours smudge, everything doubles, warps.

I come back. They're clapping.

I hear, 'Reactor, Reactor . . .'

I try saying, '*Fit your own mask first* . . .' and no one hears.

The medics are helping me up, getting under my shoulders.

I am pissing.

And I am pissing.

It's warm and plentiful.

My eyes fill with tears.

There is a glory here, full on glory.

Being me, right now, is glorious.

They're cheering the pissing, the fully soaked jeans, the trail I'm leaving as they're dragging me away.

Fuck, but didn't I hold it right to the end.

And now, problem over, job done, my body is pissing itself all over the show.

I am pissing right here and now, right on Twitter, right on YouTube, right here and now, all over the world.

I see Ratface walking backwards and shouting into my face and my hearing goes, like I've gone underwater, like I've gone for a swim.

He's mouthing, 'You – are – fucking – unstoppable!'

I've got this huge bed, this huge bed that's fit for the richest man you know. I can lie in the centre of it and I can't roll out. I can lie in the centre of it and do anything I want. I got this king-size bed with rubber sheets on it, and it's like I'm free as a bird when I'm on it. I'm lying on it now, my arms outstretched, thinking everything I can.

I was taken away by the medics, they must have checked me out, then I was brought home, dumped back in my own bed, some bandage on my head, some tube in my side. I don't need to know the details.

It's not a bad life.

Crystal won't sleep in the same bed with me, but it's not a bad life.

She's in the room next door. Ratface and Nap have the upstairs.

It's not a bad house, not a bad life.

Crystal told me in Nice that night how she'd been visited by two hotshot lawyers from Saudi, how they'd stopped her money. She said she was broke by the time we arrived in Monte Carlo.

'They got all of it?' I said.

'Yeah,' she said. 'Very nearly. They got his phone.'

'Eh?'

'His phone, Baker. Jack Melody's phone. Jack had filmed himself with me. Fucking. My husband's family got his phone in the post. They had evidence that I was an unfaithful wife, didn't qualify for his money.'

She said those million-dollar lawyers from Saudi and had been blunt during a short meeting at her Monaco hotel.

'Oh yeah, I bet,' I told her. 'How'd they get the phone?'

'I don't know,' she said. 'Who had it? Did you have it, did your coach, did Nap?'

I go, 'I don't think so. None of us, as far as I know.'

She goes, 'It was someone's little slice of revenge, whoever it was. To drop me from being about to get billions to getting nothing was revenge, I suppose.'

She looks at me and wipes an eye and goes, 'Can't blame them really, whoever it was.'

She says the hotshot lawyers gave her a few thousand in pity money, had her sign a rock solid confidentiality clause, sent her packing, tail between her legs, tucked under a kicked arse.

'So you're flat broke,' I told her. 'And poker is the new career . . .'

I had rounded up Nap and Ratface for what was a pretty tense meeting. We needed Crystal to clear us, she needed us to make our peace with her.

We braved it to Madrid and told the cops how psychotic Jack

Melody tried to kill us all. We said he'd gone for me, Nap, Ratface, Crystal.

We said Nine Hearts and the Sheikh died trying to save us, how I'd touched that murder weapon just one time in my life, and that was after the boss was dead.

Crystal told them she was withdrawing her claim I'd attacked her, that it was bullshit, that she had stolen my junk on a night at the Gaudí house, that she'd been lost in her love for Melody, that she'd said anything he wanted her to say.

A couple of Irish lawyers got involved, a couple of guys who knew my dad. They did some pro bono for us. In time, it all got cleaned up, cleaned up as much as a stink gets clean, as much as a bad mess gets clean.

In London now and I've been kicking the shit out of this sport. The fans like the back story, the danger that goes with me, the sinker with the widowed model on his arm, with the gaps in his life, with the blackouts filled with money and murder.

I'm as hot as property gets in this cold, dead game these days.

We do okay for cash, I reckon.

Ratface coaches me and a couple of younger guys, touches an arse the odd time. I train and drink and avoid sycophantic phone calls from those dildos at the PDA. I sit around and keep on making those plans to quit and do whatever.

Crystal entertains the odd wheeler dealer, the odd snapper or mucky journo, the odd low-rent oil baron. Some Arabs fly in sometimes just to hang out with her, to chat with her, to ask her about the great Sheikh Alam.

He's greatly missed, they all say.

A couple of them have fucked her, I reckon. A couple of the richer ones.

Nap still bows, escorts people in and out of our house and hasn't decked anyone yet.

Crystal gives me the odd hand job, lets me smell her breasts now and then.

It's all good.

I'm happy.

I hear what might be screwing next door now, right as I'm lying here, my bed soaked, the sun coming up on a fresh new day.

I hear her offering a few sordid words in Arabic, her little bit of extra on the side.

She's maybe wearing her black number, got her hair all covered, maybe being the Arab princess for some hopeless little sheikh, for some balloon who feels rich when he touches her.

I hear little yellow-skinned Ratface moving above now, scurrying around in his room, desperate to get into the new morning. Many of his days begin with a search of YouTube, his ongoing hunt for footage of Jack Melody hurtling through the sky. He's convinced someone must have filmed a man flying over Mallorca. He tells me he'll die happy when he sees it.

He tells me, 'I'll send that damn video to every email address on earth.'

But today he's got to get up and out for some bullshit early meeting he and Nap have arranged.

The pair of them are meeting some guy, some movie producer, some idea they've come up with about . . . what was it . . . Sherlock Holmes and Hercule Poirot and Lieutenant Columbo all in the same murder mystery.

Some shite like that.

Some oul fanny like that.

The light catches the wall shelf dead ahead of me.

We call this room the Trophy Room, the place where I sleep, where I get dumped into, the place with the bed with the built-in en suite, the place where the piss and shit and blood and puke and bits of memory from the day before can all safely blend into one and drain away.

It's the room where I rebuild what I have to wreck again.

And the soft dawn glow lights up the cups, the golden glasses, the three chunks of trinket and triumph I've managed to win in the last, hard, bastard eighteen months.

The Northern Ireland Tournament Cup – they call it the Mad Lad.

The London Championship Trophy – they call it the Throne Kicker.

And the big one, the Big Gold Bottle, the shining symbol of my greatest achievement . , , the World Championship Trophy.

They call it the World Championship Trophy.

And I'm smiling for as long as I can remember smiling.

And I'm thinking, 'Keep 'er lit, Baker. Keep 'er lit, my man . . .'